MYSTERY LADY

I settled into a seat and stared down at the stage, imagining myself there, acting, singing, gracefully dancing.

Suddenly I caught my breath. Someone *was* dancing down there.

It was her!

Leaning forward, I watched as the shimmering figure of the Woman in White glided across the stage. She had her arms raised, as if she were dancing with some invisible partner. But she was alone. And she looked sad. Very, very sad.

I should have been scared, I suppose. But I didn't sense any evil in this ghost.

So I wasn't frightened at all—until a huge hand clamped down on my shoulder.

Then I nearly fainted.

Bantam Skylark Books of related interest
Ask your bookseller for the books you have missed

ALL THE LIVING
   by Claudia Mills
A WHOLE SUMMER OF WEIRD SUSAN
   by Louise Ladd
JANET HAMM NEEDS A DATE FOR THE
   DANCE
   by Eve Bunting
THE AGAINST TAFFY SINCLAIR CLUB
   by Betsy Haynes
TAFFY SINCLAIR STRIKES AGAIN
   by Betsy Haynes
TAFFY SINCLAIR, QUEEN OF THE SOAPS
   by Betsy Haynes
TAFFY SINCLAIR AND THE ROMANCE
   MACHINE DISASTER
   by Betsy Haynes
ALICE WHIPPLE, FIFTH-GRADE DETECTIVE
   by Laurie Adams and Allison Coudert
THE GREAT MOM SWAP
   by Betsy Haynes

THE GHOST IN THE THIRD ROW

Bruce Coville

A BANTAM SKYLARK BOOK®
TORONTO · NEW YORK · LONDON · SYDNEY · AUCKLAND

RL 5, 008–012

THE GHOST IN THE THIRD ROW
A Bantam Skylark Book / July 1987

*Skylark is a registered trademark of Bantam Books, Inc.
Registered in U.S. Patent and Trademark Office and
elsewhere.*

ISBN 0-553-15519-9

Published simultaneously in the United States and Canada

---

*Bantam Books are published by Bantam Books, Inc. Its trade-
mark, consisting of the words "Bantam Books" and the por-
trayal of a rooster, is Registered in U.S. Patent and Trademark
Office and in other countries. Marca Registrada. Bantam
Books, Inc., 666 Fifth Avenue, New York, New York 10103.*

PRINTED IN THE UNITED STATES OF AMERICA

S   0 9 8 7 6 5 4 3 2 1

TO ANGIE
WHO TAKES MY WORDS
AND TURNS THEM INTO SONGS

CHAPTER ONE

Audition Blues

"Pat the elephant," said my father as we walked through the doors of the Grand Theater. "It'll bring you luck."

I looked at him like he was crazy. Not because I don't believe in doing things for luck. I do them all the time. But my dad usually makes fun of me when I tell him about them.

"Is this *my* father speaking?" I asked.

He grinned. "It's something we did when I was a kid." He walked over to the big brass elephant that stood at the side of the lobby and patted its trunk. "Like that," he said.

I copied him. I figured if I was going to survive this audition, I needed all the luck I could get.

To tell you the truth, the elephant didn't look all that lucky. Most of the brass had been rubbed away—probably by kids like me patting it for luck. Actually, the whole theater looked kind of worn down. But I could tell it had been really gorgeous when it was new. The lobby alone had more decorations than any place I'd ever seen. On the wall behind the elephant, for example, was a huge mural about twenty feet high. It looked like something from the *Arabian Nights,* with princes and genies, elephants and dancing girls. It was cracked and peeling, but I could easily imagine how beautiful it had been when it was new.

The red carpeting that covered the lobby floor was stained and worn, too, but I was sure it used to be spectacular. It swept up a big curved staircase that looked wonderful despite the chips in the gold paint and the plaster decorations. There were mirrors and chandeliers all over the place.

I found myself falling in love with the Grand, in spite of its shabbiness. Of course, it didn't hurt that my father had been raving about it for the last several weeks—ever since his architectural firm had been hired to help with a big restoration project being planned for the theater in the winter.

We walked past the staircase to a small folding table, where a girl was passing out audition forms. I took one from her, and we went into the theater itself.

It was huge.

My father told me that when he was a kid, it was the best place in Syracuse to go to the movies.

I told him I didn't think movies had been invented when he was a kid.

He said he loved me, but if I didn't shut up and fill out my audition form, he'd probably kill me.

I told him if he really felt that way he should give me a pen.

He did, and I went to work.

The form was pretty simple, really. It asked for my name (Nina Tanleven); my height (four feet, ten inches); my weight (I thought this was kind of nosy); my hair color (dark brown); and my experience (almost none, which was embarrassing).

It also asked which part I was trying out for. I didn't know, so I left that blank.

I took the form to a cranky-looking woman in the front row. She wrote a number on it, then sent me to sit with a bunch of girls at the side of the stage.

"Good luck," my dad whispered, giving me a little hug. I smiled. We had gotten pretty close since my mother left two years before. I watched fondly as he walked back a couple of rows to sit down.

I thought briefly about asking him to take me home before I made a fool of myself. I'd even promise to find something else to do for the summer. But it was too late for that now. So I took my place with the others and tried to study my music.

Another girl came and sat down beside me. She nudged me in the ribs. "Have you ever done this before?" she whispered.

I shook my head.

"Me neither," she said. "I'm so scared I could puke."

That made me feel better. I introduced myself, and she told me her name was Chris. We compared notes on how nervous we were, tore apart the other kids as they tried out, and decided the director was just too gorgeous to be real.

It didn't seem like that much time had gone by before the woman in the front row called, "Next!" and Chris was digging her elbow into my ribs and hissing, "That's you!"

I stood up and looked out at the stage.

I don't know how it did it, but I swear the thing had grown while I was waiting. It had been a normal-size stage just a little while before. Now it looked about the size of a football field!

I swallowed hard and thought about running for the door. Maybe if I was lucky, no one would remember what I looked like. My stomach tried to crawl its way into my throat, and I decided this audition was the dumbest idea I had had in years.

Then I spotted my father sitting in the third row. He smiled and gave me the thumbs-up sign.

I couldn't leave. I'd rather have hot needles stuck under my fingernails than let him down.

I took a deep breath and walked out on the stage.

"Name?" the director said.

"Nine."

The director was tall and slim, with tousled black hair. I was working hard on not developing an instant crush on him. Developing crushes was this stupid thing that had started happening to me in the last year.

I wasn't having much luck.

He raised one eyebrow. He came close to making an actual question mark out of it. *"Nine?"* he asked.

"Well, it's really Nina. But everyone calls me Nine, because my last name is Tanleven."

He didn't say anything.

"Get it?" I asked hopefully. "Nine Tan-Leven?"

Inside me a little voice was yelling, "Shut up, stupid."

As usual, I ignored it and just babbled on. "See, I've been stuck with it since first grade and—"

Mr. Director (I found out later his name was Edgar, so I don't know what he thought was so bad about Nine anyway) held up his hand to stop me. "What are you going to sing for us—Nine?"

I bit my lip and wished I were dead. I had brought the music for "Tomorrow," from *Annie*. So had almost every other girl who had sung before me.

I told him. He was very nice. The corners of his mouth twitched a little, but that was about the only sign he gave of what he must have been thinking.

I handed the music to the pianist, who probably knew it by heart by then anyway, and took my place to sing.

Once I started, I didn't care how many times Cute Edgar had heard the song that day. I loved singing it.

And I was good.

I'm not claiming I'll be the next Julie Andrews. But I do have two things I can do well. Sing and run. (Nina Tanleven, the singing sprinter, that's me.) I think they're connected—strong lungs, if you know what I mean.

As I started the second verse I looked out at my father to see how I was doing. I almost choked on a high note.

There was a woman sitting next to him.

Yeah, I know, that's not all that strange. He's thirty-six, and not bad looking for a father. But the woman was wearing a dress that belonged somewhere around the turn of the century.

Even that's not so strange. She might have been in costume for another show. But here's the really amazing thing: it seemed like I could see right through her!

Now that was strange.

I dropped a note, forced myself to concentrate on the song, and when I looked back she was gone.

I hoped I would find her later. It wasn't fair to startle me like that when I was auditioning. My song had been going great until then, and I wanted to tell her off.

"Thank you," Edgar said. "That's enough!"

And I was just getting warmed up! I figured I must have really blown it. You can imagine how surprised I was a week later when I got the call telling me I had a part in the show.

I thought my troubles were over.

Boy, was I wrong!

CHAPTER TWO

The Woman in White

I had another attack of nerves when my father dropped me off for the first rehearsal. I considered just going to the coffee shop down the street and hanging out until it was time for him to pick me up. But I was pretty sure that after a while someone would call my house to find out where I was, and I'd end up in trouble.

So I took a deep breath and walked in.

The cast members were being sent to a group of rickety wooden chairs that had been set in a

8

half-circle on the stage, facing the audience. Only there wasn't any audience—just a long table at the edge of the stage where the production crew sat facing us. Cute Edgar was sitting in the center. To his right was the cranky-looking woman who had taken my audition form. Her name was Gwendolyn Meyer, and it turned out she was our producer. To Edgar's left was the girl who had handed me the audition form. She was going to be our stage manager. Her name was Heidi, and I wanted to kill her.

It wasn't that Heidi had actually done anything to me. It was just that she was beautiful, and I didn't care to have anyone that pretty sitting next to Edgar.

At the end of the table sat a kind of nice-looking guy with big brown eyes. Next to him was a very pretty red-haired woman. The man turned out to be Alan Bland—yuck, what an awful name—who had written the script and lyrics for the show we were going to do. The lady was his partner, Paula Geller. She had written the music and would also be coaching the singers and conducting the orchestra for the performances.

At that moment Cute Edgar was going on about how lucky we were to be able to present the world premiere of this play, which was called *The Woman in White* and was based on an event that had taken place in the very theater where we were going to perform it!

"Lucky," said a husky voice next to me.

I glanced to my right, where a golden-haired girl named Melissa Clayton was sitting. Melissa was a year or two older than me. But since the audition notice had specifically called for "three girls in the ten to thirteen age group," I had a feeling we were going to end up working together.

"If this dog is any good, why are they premiering it here instead of in a real theater?" Melissa continued.

I wanted to tell her that the Grand *was* a real theater. But I knew what she meant. Who was there in Syracuse, New York, who could see our show and make any difference?

So I kept my mouth shut.

That didn't stop Melissa. All the time Edgar was talking, she whispered on and on about how stupid everything was. I wanted to reach over and pinch her lips together and then ask her why she was there if she didn't like it.

I found out later there were two reasons: one, Melissa wanted to be a star; and two, Melissa's mother *really* wanted her to be a star.

It was clear she was going to be a royal pain. The good news was that the third girl was none other than Chris Gurley, who I had been talking to at auditions. She had come in late—I learned later it was a habit with her—and she was sitting on the other side of me.

Edgar had finished talking and was just about to pass out the scripts when an old man appeared at the edge of the stage.

"Hey, Pop!" cried Edgar, jumping to his feet.

I was confused for a moment. This guy seemed way too old to be Edgar's father.

As it turned out, Pop was just the man's nickname. He was in charge of keeping the theater in shape. After Edgar introduced him, Pop gave a few rules: "No smoking, no drinks in the audience area, no gum under the seats . . ." Then he shuffled away to a smattering of applause.

"What an old fart," said Melissa.

"Shhh!" hissed Chris, who was sitting on the other side of me. She had kept quiet until then, but I could tell she had been dying to tell Melissa to shut up.

Melissa's eyes flashed, and I knew instantly that it wouldn't be a good idea to get stuck between her and Chris any more than necessary.

As he was passing out the scripts, Edgar asked Alan Bland to give us a little background on the story. Alan said it was about a tragic romance that had taken place in the Grand Theater some fifty years ago. In those days Syracuse was a major tryout town for shows heading for New York City. One of the great stars of that time, a beautiful actress named Lily Larkin, had come here with a big costume drama that looked like it was going to be a smash hit when it finally got to Broadway.

Two of the troupe's actors, Edward Parker and Andrew Heron, had fallen in love with Lily. Both men had been courting her all through the tour, but only one man had been successful. Lily Larkin had fallen in love with Edward Parker. When the troupe reached Syracuse, Lily and Edward announced their engagement to the cast.

After Lily chose Edward, Andrew Heron decided if he couldn't have her, no one could. During the next night's performance, he climbed into the rigging, cut a rope, and sent a huge chandelier hurtling toward the stage. It struck Lily while she was in the middle of her big song, a romantic ballad with the same title as the show: "The Heart That Stays True."

Lily fell to the floor. Moments later she died in the arms of her true love, Edward Parker.

Since that night, according to the legend, Lily's ghost had haunted the theater where she died—the very theater we were sitting in!

As Alan spoke, I could feel the hair on the back of my neck begin to rise. Not because it was a good story—although I thought it was. Not because I was sitting in a cold draft, although that was true, too. The reason the hair on the back of my neck was standing up was simple: the woman Alan Bland was describing was the woman who had been sitting next to my father on the day of the auditions.

I had actually seen the ghost of Lily Larkin!

CHAPTER THREE

Lydia the Leading Lady

At first I didn't say anything about what I had seen during the auditions. I didn't think anyone would believe me. I wasn't even sure I believed it myself.

But just a few nights later, two things happened to make me change my mind and tell all. . . .

It was our third night of real rehearsals. Edgar had sent Chris, Melissa, and me to a little room on the second floor of the theater, to learn our big second-act song.

14

Paula Geller, the composer, was working with us. I was really excited at first, because she had assigned each of us a solo. Then I found out I just couldn't sing my part right!

After my fifth try, Paula raised her fingers from the keyboard and looked at me over the top of her glasses. "You're a trifle flat," she said.

"Of course she's flat," whispered Melissa. "She's only eleven!"

Melissa was *only* twelve herself, but she was built like she was fourteen—at least.

Pow! I thought, sending a mental blast in her direction. If mental telepathy really worked, I would have fried her brains.

Unfortunately, it had no effect. But out of the corner of my eye, I saw Chris give her the elbow.

Good old Chris. At least I had one friend in the room!

Paula pushed back the strand of damp red hair hanging over her eyes and let out a little sigh. "Let's try it again, Nine," she said slowly.

I wasn't sure whether she was sighing because of my singing or Melissa's wisecracks. I imagine they were both a little hard to take on a hot summer night in a cramped room with no air-conditioning.

"Breathe more deeply this time," Paula said as she began pounding the keys again.

What am I doing here? I wondered desperately. *I can't do this!* I was beginning to get the feeling that pretty soon I would be asked to leave.

Of course, Melissa's comments weren't helping any. I really thought I could do what Paula wanted if I could just relax. But who can relax with a beady-eyed blonde waiting for you to make a mistake so she can laugh about it?

I wondered if it wouldn't have been smarter to let my father plan my summer for me after all.

"Yoo-hoo," said Paula. "Are you there, Nine?"

I blushed. I had gotten so distracted that I missed my cue.

I took a deep breath and nodded my head. Paula began to play again. Remembering a trick my chorus teacher had taught me, I tried to imagine the note I kept messing up coming out clear and bell-like.

The note was only two measures away. I belted out the words "on the stage!" and reached for the note as if my life depended on it.

I was lucky it didn't; I would have been dead on the spot.

Paula put her head on the keyboard and groaned. Melissa snorted. I could feel a blush creeping up my cheeks.

"You'd better work on it at home for a while," said Paula softly.

I wanted to crawl under a rock and die.

Just then Edgar came bounding into the room. He had a pencil tucked behind one ear, and he was carrying a clipboard. "Well," he said, "how goes it, troops?"

He looked so eager and enthusiastic I couldn't bear for him to find out I was letting him down.

"Scram, Edgar," said Paula in a tired voice. "We're not ready for you to hear us yet."

"In fact, we probably never will be," whispered Melissa.

I thought it would be nice if the ceiling fell in on her right then.

Edgar's smile faded a little. "Paula," he said, "we're using this number for the radio spot. It has to be ready by next week!"

I thought Paula was going to explode. "Next week?" she screeched. "The show doesn't open for nearly two months! Now you listen to me, Edgar Lonis—"

Paula's tirade was interrupted by a scream from the hallway.

I had heard kids scream on the playground all my life. And I'd heard scream queens in the movies. But that was the first time I had ever heard a real-life scream of terror. I thought my skin was going to crawl right off my body.

Have you ever been watching a movie when they stop the projector but keep the picture on the screen? For a minute everyone just freezes in some weird position. Then the projector starts again, and everyone bounces into action.

It was like that in the little rehearsal room. For a minute after we heard that scream, no one moved at all. Then everyone bolted for the door. Chris and I were the last ones through. Melissa was first, naturally. A small crowd had already gathered in the hall by the time we got there.

"Stand back! Give her air!" That was Edgar, trying to push his way through the cluster of actors and production people.

As they moved aside, I could see who had been screaming. It was Lydia Crane, the beautiful woman who had the starring role in the show.

Lydia was stretched out on the floor. Alan Bland, Paula's writing partner, was kneeling behind Lydia. He had placed her head on his knees. Ken Abbott, the handsome, dark-haired leading man, was bending over her, patting her cheek as though he was trying to wake her up.

Lydia's eyes were wide open, but I had the feeling she wasn't seeing any of us. It was almost as if she was looking into another world.

Edgar reached down and put his hand on her arm. First she flinched away from him; then she turned and looked into his eyes.

"The Woman in White," she whispered. Her voice was husky with fear. The sound of it made the little hairs on the back of my neck stand up. "Edgar, it was the Woman in White!"

She buried her face in her hands and began to sob.

CHAPTER FOUR

The View from the Balcony

Do you know what *frisson* means?

If you do, you're ahead of me. I only learned it because my fifth-grade teacher used it all the time. He was a true horror-movie freak, and he decided if a film was any good by whether or not it provoked a frisson in him. Anyway, it's a word the French came up with to describe that tingle that skitters down your spine and across your skin when something truly horrifying happens.

Frisson is the word I always think of when I remember the look in Lydia's eyes that night. At one point she turned her face directly toward me. But I know she didn't see me. It was as if she were looking into some bottomless pit.

That's when the frisson hit me. It was like thousands of little ants running across my skin.

Poor Alan Bland was almost as bad off as Lydia. His big eyes were wide with fright, and his bony hands trembled as he tried to hold her up.

Paula knelt by his side and put a hand on his shoulder. "Did you see it, too?" she asked.

Alan shook his head no. His mouth opened and closed a few times, and his Adam's apple bobbed up and down in his throat. But no sound came out.

Melissa nudged me in the ribs. "What a nerd," she whispered loudly.

Paula shot us a sharp glance.

I wanted to die of embarrassment—and I hadn't even said anything! Right about then I would have handed Melissa over to the ghost without a second thought.

Suddenly a booming voice cried out, "What in hell is going on here?" Looking up, I saw Gwendolyn Meyer pushing her way through the knot of people surrounding Lydia. Ken Abbott quickly moved out of her way.

"Lydia thought she saw something," Edgar said quietly. "It frightened her."

Gwendolyn rolled her eyes. "Don't tell me," she said sarcastically. "Let me guess. Our famous ghost has made another appearance, and our leading lady has become faint-hearted and collapsed."

"Gwendolyn," said Edgar, in a warning tone.

But Gwendolyn was wound up and ready to roll. Her nostrils flared, making her look a little like a racehorse. "Actresses!" she snorted. "Someday I'd like to produce a series of plays without a single actress in them. I get so tired of whining, sniveling—"

"Gwendolyn!" snapped Edgar. "Back off!"

Gwendolyn reared back, a ferocious look on her face. But she closed her mouth.

"What's bugging *her*?" Chris whispered as Edgar and Alan helped Lydia to her feet.

"Oh, she's always that way," whispered Melissa knowingly.

"All right, why don't we get back to work?" said Edgar. "We've got plenty to do!"

Muttering among themselves, the cast and crew began to drift away. Chris, Melissa, and I lingered on because Paula was still talking to Alan.

"You girls had better go back to the room," she said, suddenly noticing us. "I'll be there in a minute."

Reluctantly, we turned to go. As we did, I noticed that the only other person still standing in the hall was Pop.

He didn't see me looking at him because he was staring at Lydia. I don't know what he was thinking. But the look in his eyes sent another frisson skittering down my back.

I turned and hurried after the others.

"Well," said Paula when she joined us back in our rehearsal room. "That was certainly exciting. I had no idea Alan and I would be stirring up such nonsense when we wrote this show."

"Nonsense?" said Chris. She sounded really surprised. "Do you mean you don't believe in the ghost?"

Paula snorted. "How dumb do I look?" she asked. "Bite your tongues," she said before any of us could answer.

I smiled. She had said it to all of us. But she was looking directly at Melissa.

Not that it did any good. Melissa opened her mouth anyway. To my surprise, she asked a halfway intelligent question. "If you don't believe in the ghost, why did you ask Alan if he saw it?"

Paula began to blush. "I—I just wanted to know if he had seen something that might have looked like a ghost," she said. "I assumed there was something that Lydia took for a ghost. I thought he might know what it was."

I didn't believe her for a minute. Neither did the others. "She was lying through her teeth" was the way Chris expressed it when we were standing outside the theater waiting for our parents to pick us up.

Before I could ask her why she felt that way a battered blue Volkswagen bumped into the curb in front of us. "That's my dad," said Chris. "I've got to go. See you tomorrow night." She scrambled into the car and rolled down the window. "Assuming the ghost doesn't get you first!" she cried as her father began to pull away. Then she tried to laugh a deep, spooky laugh. Only it came out more like a cackle.

I was alone in front of the theater. Actually, Melissa was standing beside me. But as far as I was concerned, that still meant I was without human company.

To my surprise, she actually spoke to me. "I've got my lines all memorized," she said. "Do you?"

Before I could answer, a silver BMW slid in next to the curb. Without waiting for me to answer her question, Melissa walked to the car. I thought she was going to leave without even saying goodbye. But just as she was about to get into the car, she turned to me and said, "Try sneaking a breath two beats before that note you're having trouble with. It might help."

She slid into the car and slammed the door before I could say either "Thank you" or "Bug off," which were the two responses I was considering. The BMW pulled out into traffic.

As I was standing there, it started to rain. I was tired. I was hungry. And I had to go to the bathroom.

"Come on, Dad," I said, bouncing on one foot and then the other. "Get me out of this place."

He didn't come.

Five minutes went by, and he still hadn't come. I was starting to feel as if I might explode.

I looked back through the glass doors of the theater. A few people still lingered inside the lobby. I could see Edgar, Gwendolyn, Paula, and Alan. They seemed to be arguing about something. I didn't want to intrude. But I *had* to use the bathroom.

Moving quietly, I slipped through the doors and headed for the stairway that led up to the bathrooms. Nobody seemed to notice me.

The mezzanine where the bathrooms were located was like half a second floor. Part of it was cut away, and it was surrounded by a railing, so I could look down into the lobby.

I wasn't too thrilled by the fact that the lights were out up there. But by sticking to the railing, I got enough light from the lower level to see where I was going. Trying to kind of glide along, so I wouldn't make too much noise, I passed above the group on the first floor.

"Not good for the cast!" I heard Edgar saying. His voice was low, but fierce. I was dying to stop there and eavesdrop for a while. But I had to get to the bathroom!

The lights were out there, too. But once I was inside the door, it took only a moment of fumbling to find the switch.

If I had had any common sense, I would have taken care of my business, run back down the stairs, and headed for the street. But common sense was never one of my strong points. At least, that was what my mother had always claimed, before she left. So she probably wouldn't have been surprised at what happened after I left the bathroom.

The funny thing is, it still surprises *me*. I mean, I'm not usually all that bold and brave. And when you consider what had already happened in the theater that night, I should have been shaking all over. But when I spotted that little sign over the door that led to the balcony, I just couldn't resist sneaking up to take a look. I had admired the balcony from the stage the first night of rehearsals. I also knew it was off-limits, except when the theater had some attraction that really packed the house.

I figured I might never have a better chance to see it. Even so, I hesitated for a moment, wondering if my father had gotten there yet. But then I decided that I had had to wait for him, so it wouldn't hurt him to wait another minute or two for me.

Taking a deep breath, I stepped through the door.

The stairwell was dark and surprisingly cool, considering what a hot night it was. Keeping one hand against the wall, I made my way slowly up the short flight of stairs.

The carpeting muffled my footsteps. The theater seemed deathly still.

I was tingling with excitement, and for a moment I had the feeling I was headed for some wonderful adventure—that maybe when I had traveled through this strange, dark passage I would come out in some totally different world.

Sometimes my imagination gets out of control.

Naturally I was disappointed when I reached the balcony and discovered that it was, after all, only a balcony.

But only a *little* disappointed. Because it was wonderful being up there. By the dim light filtering up from the stage area, I could see great long rows of seats stretching in front of me. To my right the rows marched upward, rising until they were lost out of sight in the darkness at the top of the theater.

When I turned left, toward the stage, it was even more wonderful. The theater was stretched out beneath me like some glorious, oversize dollhouse. The modern movie theaters I go to suddenly seemed bare and tiny compared to this space.

I settled into a seat and stared down at the stage, imagining myself there, acting, singing, gracefully dancing.

Suddenly I caught my breath. Someone *was* dancing down there.

It was her!

Leaning forward, I held my breath and watched as the shimmering figure of the Woman in White glided across the stage. She was wearing that same old-fashioned dress, which I now realized must be the costume she had been wearing when she was killed. She had her arms raised, as if she were dancing with some invisible partner. But she was alone. And she looked sad. Very, very sad.

From somewhere, I heard the faintest strain of music.

At first I could barely make it out. But after a moment I recognized it as a song Paula had played for us earlier in the evening. It was "The Heart That Stays True"—the song Lily Larkin had been singing when she was murdered.

I should have been scared, I suppose. But I didn't sense any evil in this ghost. Just terrible loneliness.

So I wasn't frightened at all—until a huge hand clamped down on my shoulder.

Then I nearly fainted.

CHAPTER FIVE

Chris

Three things happened at once: I started to scream; I spun around in my seat; and I heard a familiar voice snarling, "What are you doing up here, kid?"

It was Pop. He looked fierce, not at all like the sweet old grandfatherly type I had imagined him to be.

I swallowed and looked back toward the stage. The ghost was gone.

Had he seen her?

"I said, what are you doing up here?" repeated Pop, giving me a little shake. I turned back to him. There was anger in his eyes—and something else, too. Only I couldn't figure out what it was.

"I—I just came up to look," I stammered. "I wasn't hurting anything."

"Well, just get yourself right back down," said Pop gruffly. "This balcony is off-limits to anyone who doesn't have a ticket—which is most people, most of the time. You kids get to sneaking up here and the next thing you know one of you will be falling over the edge. Then your parents will be suing the theater because we didn't keep you out of here! They ought to sue themselves for not teaching you better manners! Go on! Scat!"

I got out of there as fast as I could, racing down the stairs so quickly I nearly made Pop's prediction about hurting myself come true. I shot across the mezzanine, down the next flight of stairs, through the lobby, and out the front doors—something like the Cowardly Lion running away from the Wizard of Oz, except that I opened the door instead of going through the glass.

My father was just pulling up to the curb.

"Well, looks like my timing was perfect," he said cheerfully as I quickly got into the car. "They must have put you through some workout tonight, Nine. You're all out of breath!"

If he only knew, I thought.

Lydia and I had seen the ghost on Wednesday night. There was another rehearsal scheduled for the next evening. But by ten o'clock on Thursday morning I was so desperate to talk to somebody about what I had seen that I thought I would go out of my mind waiting.

Finally I decided to call Chris. It took me six calls because there were over a dozen Gurleys in the phone book, and I had no idea where she lived. I just started at the top of the list and worked my way down. No answer at the first two, an old lady at the third, no answer at the fourth, and a *very* cranky man at the fifth. He said he worked nights and I had woken him up. He also said several other things, but I had better not put them on paper.

I was about ready to give up after the episode with Mr. Cranky. But then I remembered my grandmother's saying that people who gave up on something with less than a hundred tries didn't deserve to succeed anyway. That always seemed a bit on the high side to me, but I figured five was really on the low side. So I tried again.

"Hello, this is the Gurley residence," said Chris.

Bingo! "Chris," I said. "This is Nine."

Chris ignored me and kept right on talking. "This is Bonk, the cat, speaking. No one else is available now, so the folks have put me in charge of the phone."

An answering machine. I hate answering machines!

"At the sound of my meow, please leave your name and message. I'll make sure it gets to the right person. Also, please let me know if you have any spare mice."

There were a couple of seconds of whirring noise, then a loud meow.

I almost said, "This is Nine. I saw the ghost. Call me as soon as you can!"

Fortunately, I caught myself in time. If Chris's parents got to the answering machine before she did, they'd think I had really freaked out.

"This is Nine," I said. "I need to—"

I was interrupted by a clicking sound. "Nine! How are you?"

"Chris?"

"You were expecting maybe the Woman in White?"

"Don't say that!" I snapped.

"Hey, what's going on? You sound grouchy enough to be Melissa!"

"Don't ever say that to me," I said. "You startled me, that's all. Anyway, why do you have your answering machine on if you're at home?"

"To filter calls, dummy. What if it had been Melissa, instead of you? I haven't had breakfast yet. I don't think I could stand to talk to her on an empty stomach this early in the morning."

"Chris, it's almost noon."

"So shoot me. It's summer and I like to get up late. Did you want something, or did you just call to nag me?"

"No, I need to talk to you."

"Go ahead."

Suddenly I felt really stupid. "Can we get together somehow? I don't want to talk about it on the phone."

"Why not?" asked Chris. "Is it dirty?"

"No, it's not dirty! I just don't want to talk about it on the phone!"

"Can you get downtown?"

Downtown itself was easy; the bus came right by my house every fifteen minutes or so. Getting permission was another matter.

"I'll have to call my father at work and ask him. You'd better be flattered. I'll probably have to endure a ten-minute lecture on the dangers of downtown before he lets me go."

"Better you than me. I'll wait for your call."

Chris was standing in front of the library when I got there.

I smiled when I saw her. Not because she looked funny, or even because she looked pretty, though the fact is, she was both, which isn't easy. I smiled because that's the kind of person she is. She just makes you want to smile.

I waved when I spotted her. I expected her to wave back, but she acted as if I didn't exist.

I thought maybe she had decided she was angry at me for dragging her down there to talk, instead of just telling her my problem over the phone. I figured I'd better apologize as soon as possible.

"Look, Chris, I'm sorry about—"

She cut me off with a fierce hiss. "Shhhhh!" She looked around, then squinted at me. "Follow me!" she whispered. "Ve vill go vhere no one can hear us!" She was speaking in a ridiculous German accent and arching one eyebrow like a bad actor playing a spy in an old movie.

Taking my arm, she led me across the street to a little plaza filled with pigeons and hot-dog vendors.

We crossed the plaza and headed down a narrow side street that went off in an odd direction. About halfway to the next block, Chris cut into a parking lot. At one side of the parking lot, looking totally out of place, was a large tree. Chris scrambled up the trunk, sat down on one of the branches, and motioned for me to follow.

"What are you acting so mysterious about?" I asked when I had managed to struggle my way up the tree. I'm about three inches shorter than Chris; it's not much, but there are times when every inch counts.

"Me?" she said indignantly. She scowled, then switched back to her sophisticated German act. "My darlink, am I ze one who called and begged to talk wiz someone, zen refused to tell someone vat it vas all about? Oh, no, no! Not I. It vas *you* who indicated a need for secrecy. I am zimply tryink to provide it."

I smiled. "That's pretty good," I said. "How long did it take you to get it down pat?"

"Forget that!" said Chris, dropping the accent. "Tell me what this is all about before I get really impatient and push you out of this tree."

I blushed. Out there in the open, with the sun shining so brightly, the whole thing seemed totally silly. Suddenly I understood why ghost stories work better in the dark.

"Come on, Nine," said Chris impatiently. "What's up? Do you have a crush on Cute Edgar or something?"

I could feel my blush spreading. "I told you this was serious!" I said, sidestepping her question.

"Well, what is it?"

I took a deep breath. "I saw the ghost last night."

Chris's eyes flashed angrily. She started to climb out of the tree. " Nine, if you dragged me all the way down here to—"

"Chris!" I said desperately. "I'm not kidding! I saw her. And it was the second time!"

I don't know if it was something in my voice or if she had just started to leave for effect, but now she looked at me and said, "You're not kidding, are you?"

"Chris, I had to promise to do dishes for a week to get my father to let me come down here. Now would I do that for a joke?"

"Not unless you're dumber than you look," said Chris, climbing back up beside me.

We sat in silence for a moment. "Well," Chris said finally. "What a relief that is."

"Huh?" I asked, sounding less than intelligent.

"I'm just so glad you saw her. I thought maybe I was going out of my mind."

"What are you talking about?" I asked.

Chris looked at me. "Isn't it obvious?" she said. "I saw the ghost, too!"

CHAPTER SIX

The Hunk in the Reference Room

"Whoa, girl," yelled Chris, grabbing my arm to steady me on the branch. She did this because I nearly fell out of the tree when she told me she had seen the ghost, too. I had never thought about anyone else seeing it.

"Take it easy, Nine," said Chris. "You look like—sorry about this—you look like you just saw a ghost. What's the matter? Didn't you want me to see her? Were you planning on keeping her all to yourself?"

"No. It's just that—Well, why didn't you say something before?"

"Why didn't *you*?" Chris asked logically.

"I don't know. I was afraid no one would believe me. I thought they would laugh at me."

"So do I look that different from you?" she asked. "You think I want the rest of the cast to decide I've got a screw loose?"

Suddenly a nasty thought crossed my mind. Was Chris just pretending to have seen the ghost? "What did she look like when you saw her?" I asked, testing her.

Chris paused for a moment. "Well," she said at last, "she was pretty. Very pretty. I remember that she had a long slender neck and high cheekbones."

I nodded. What she said was true, but it was too general. I wanted more details. "What was she wearing?"

"She had on a very old-fashioned dress," said Chris, "with those funny kind of sleeves—you know, the ones that are all puffy at the top, and then tight from the wrist to the elbow. And she was wearing several strings of pearls around her neck."

The pearls did it. They weren't in the script, and they weren't the kind of detail someone would think of if they hadn't really seen the ghost. "That's right!" I said excitedly. "That's just the way she looked when I saw her."

"Well, of course it's the way she looked when you saw her," said Chris. "You don't think she changes her clothes, do you? She's wearing the costume she died in."

Suddenly I felt a little guilty for having suspected her. After all, this was Chris, not Melissa.

"Well, what do you think we should do about it?" I asked, partly to change the subject.

"Why should we do anything?" asked Chris.

"I don't know," I said. "Somehow it just seems like we ought to do something about all this."

"Why?"

"Well, because it's upsetting people. I mean, look what happened with Lydia last night."

"Do you think it would make Lydia feel better if we told her we had seen the ghost, too?"

"Yes! No. I mean—I don't know. Wouldn't it?"

"Why should it?" said Chris. "She was scared enough as it was. Though to tell you the truth, that seemed kind of weird to me. I mean, did the ghost seem scary to you?"

Chris had just put her finger on something that had been bothering me, too. "No, she didn't," I said. "She seemed sad. But not really scary."

"So what was all the screaming about last night?"

"Well, Lydia's probably kind of high-strung. And you've got to admit that the Grand is pretty spooky anyway. It probably just startled her."

"I guess you're right," said Chris. But she didn't look convinced.

"And you really don't think we should do anything about it?" I asked.

"Well, it wouldn't hurt to learn a little more about this 'Woman in White.' Just to make sure she's harmless."

"How do we do that? I've read the script five times already."

"Forget the script," Chris said, climbing down. "Alan and Paula said the script was 'based on' a true story. If that's anything like on television, I'd say it means only three things out of every hundred have to be true. Come on. Let's go back to the library."

"Why the library?" I asked, scrambling down after her.

"Research, dummy."

"I doubt there are any books about this story. It's just a local thing."

"So we look in the local newspapers."

"They save that kind of stuff?" I asked, thinking about the stacks of newspapers we threw out every month.

"They have to. It's their job." Chris was already trotting across the parking lot. "Come on!" she yelled over her shoulder. "Let's get moving!"

I, the fast sprinter, was wondering how Chris could talk so much and run so fast at the same time. She didn't slow down until we started climbing the steps to the library.

The librarian at the front desk sent us upstairs to the reference room. We had to climb a huge set of winding marble stairs to get there.

In the reference room I got the second, but not the last, major shock of my day. The librarian sitting behind the desk was a hunk! I mean, who would have thought it? Librarians are supposed to be little old ladies. OK, I'll admit a lot of them aren't little and a lot more aren't old. But how many of them are guys who look good enough to be models?

The Hunk stood up as we crossed to his desk. "Can I help you young ladies?" he asked.

"Yes," said Chris briskly. "We'd like to look—"

"At your eyes," I finished, without realizing I was speaking out loud.

Chris jabbed me in the ribs with her elbow. "At your files of local newspapers."

"In the periodical room," he said, swinging his arm to the right. We headed off in the direction he indicated.

"By the way," he called after us, "do you know how to use the microfilm reader?"

I shook my head vigorously. I hoped that if by some chance Chris had already learned how to use the thing she would have the good sense to keep her mouth shut.

"Better let me show you," he said, crossing to join us. "It's not hard, but there's no sense in wasting a lot of time trying to figure it out."

He led us into a room that seemed to contain only three kinds of things. The first things I noticed were long shelves filled with sets of books that all looked alike. I couldn't figure out why they had so many copies of each book, until I looked at their spines and realized they were magazines that had been bound into book form. I wondered for a minute why they bothered. I mean, who would want to look at a twenty-year-old copy of *Ladies' Home Journal*? But then I remembered I was here to look at a fifty-year-old local newspaper. So why not a twenty-year-old magazine?

Next I noticed dozens of squashed-looking file cabinets. Not squashed as if they had been sat on by an elephant—just squashed as in being about twice as wide and half as tall as the ones I was used to. You see people shaped like that sometimes, too. It's always a real shock.

The third things were these big glass and metal machines that looked like they had been made out of television sets and storm windows.

"Now, what year did you girls have in mind?"

We looked at each other blankly. "You just told me you've read the script five times," Chris said. "What year is it set in?"

"Script?" asked BBEG. (That's "Blond, Blue-Eyed, and Gorgeous.") "Are you girls doing a show?"

"We're in *The Woman in White,* at the Grand Theater," Chris said proudly.

Talk about magic words! It turned out that the librarian, who told us we should call him Sam, was an actor, too. I could tell that in his eyes we had suddenly been transformed from under-age nuisances to human beings. It was as if we had just found out we were part of the same family.

"I really wanted to try out for that show myself," said Sam wistfully. "I'd love to work in that old theater. But I just got this job, and they have me working three nights a week, so I could never have made rehearsals." He sighed. "Anyway, tell me who else is in the cast."

Chris started listing people, and it seemed as if Sam knew half of them. He made us tell him everything we could think of about the show and what was going on with it. Somehow, we managed to answer all his questions without letting on about the real reason we had come to the library.

We were having so much fun gossiping about the show that it was nearly half an hour before we got back to the subject of the microfilm. Actually, I was the one who got us on track again when I suddenly shouted, "July, 1935!" in a voice far too loud for the library.

Sam looked at me strangely.

"That's the date of the play," I said, blushing. "I just remembered it."

Sam was surprised we were bothering to do research for our roles. He got a bigger surprise when he opened the drawer where the microfilm for the July, 1935, Syracuse *Herald American* was supposed to be stored.

I happened to be looking over his shoulder when he pulled the drawer open. I saw about a hundred square boxes, each about an inch thick and small enough to fit in my hand. They were arranged in neat, tight rows.

It was all in order, except for the gaping hole where the July, 1935, box should have been.

Chris and I would have been disappointed, but not much more, except for one strange fact: Syracuse had four daily newspapers in 1935, and the library had complete files on all of them. Or more accurately, nearly complete files.

July, 1935, was missing from every single one of them.

CHAPTER SEVEN

Young Women Who
Love the Theater

"Time for dinner!" called my father.

Chris pushed a large orange blob of fur off her lap. It batted her leg once, then stalked away in a huff.

"Don't be a creep, Sidney," I said.

"All cats are that way," Chris said. "Come on, I'm starving."

My father had invited Chris to join us for dinner after I dragged her to his office with the promise of a ride home.

"Well, did you girls have an interesting day?" he asked now, passing a heaping platter of fried chicken to Chris.

"Very," said Chris. She gave me a sidelong glance as she forked a juicy drumstick onto her plate. "We spent a lot of time at the library."

"Wait," said my father. "Don't tell me. Let me guess. One of the librarians is a—what's that word? Oh, yes! One of the librarians is a hunk!"

"Dad!" I yelped. I blushed, partly because of what he had said and partly because it was embarrassing to have my father know me so well.

Ignoring me, he turned his attention to Chris. "And how are rehearsals going?" he asked.

She rolled her eyes. "They're interesting, too," she said. "Our leading lady saw the theater's ghost last night."

My dad was really cool. Other than raising an eyebrow, he didn't miss a beat.

"How did she take it?" he asked, his voice as calm as if we were discussing a change in Lydia's costume.

"Not too well," said Chris. "She sort of flipped out." She shot me a sideward glance and said, "To tell you the truth, Mr. Tanleven, I don't think she's very mature. When Nine and I saw the ghost, we handled it a lot more calmly than Lydia did."

I would like to be able to tell you that I stayed calm when Chris dropped that particular bomb-shell. The truth is I nearly spit a mouthful of mashed potatoes across the table. As for my father, he just raised his eyebrow a little higher.

"Is that so? I don't think Nine bothered to mention it to me."

No one said anything for a moment. The only sounds around the table were the ones that came from me trying to swallow the potatoes while I worked out a way to kill Chris without getting caught.

"I guess it must have slipped my mind," I said when I was finally able to talk again.

My father seemed to find this considerably more difficult to believe than the idea that we had seen the ghost. He didn't say anything, but I thought his eyebrow was going to twitch its way right over his forehead.

"It's quite a compliment, you know," he said at last, scooping a forkful of salad into his mouth.

It was our turn to be surprised, and he looked smug while he munched on his lettuce.

"OK!" I finally yelled. "We give up. Why is it a compliment?"

My dad shrugged. "According to the legend," he said, spearing a tomato with his fork, "the

Woman in White only appears to young women who truly love the theater. If you saw her, it must mean you qualify. There *are* worse things that could be said of a person, you know."

I was still trying to figure out a suitable way to take revenge on Chris when my father dropped us off at the theater about an hour later.

"Have you lost your marbles?" I hissed as soon as he pulled away from the curb. "If I'd known you were such a blabbermouth, I never would have let my dad invite you to dinner. What are you trying to do to me, anyway?"

"Chill out," said Chris. "Everything's fine, in case you haven't noticed."

"That's easy for you to say," I snorted. "You don't live at my house."

"Look," said Chris, "in case you're not aware of it, your father is a very cool person. I figured that out as soon as I met him. Couldn't you tell I was checking him out when I told him about Lydia seeing the ghost? When he handled that fine, I figured he could handle it if we had, too. Especially," she said, "since I made a point of saying we had *both* seen her."

"Well, what was the *point* to begin with?" I snapped. "Why couldn't you just leave well enough alone?"

She sighed. "Aside from the fact that I was being charitable—"

"Charitable?" I gasped.

"Sure. Look, Nine, I could tell it was driving you crazy to keep this from your father. I figured the best thing I could do for you was take that load off your mind."

"I'll handle my own loads, if you don't mind," I said sharply. Suddenly I thought of something. "Have you told your parents?"

Chris looked truly horrified. "Are you kidding? They'd flip out!"

"Well, you've got a lot of nerve," I said, "telling my father when—"

"But don't you see the difference?" asked Chris. "The great thing is I *could* tell your father. You don't know how lucky you are."

That slowed me down a little.

"Besides," she continued before I could think of a response, "we got the other reaction I was hoping for."

"And what was that?" I asked cautiously.

"We picked up some new information. In case you haven't figured it out yet, Knowledge is Power."

I looked at her as if she were from another planet.

"You can look at me like that if you want," she said. "The first time I saw that slogan carved on the doorway over my old school, I thought it was really stupid. Then I realized the more I knew, the more I could control what was going on around me. It's just a matter of what knowledge you want to have. Right now, we want to know as much about the ghost as possible, so we played a little trading game."

"*You* played a game," I said. "I had nothing to do with it."

"Suit yourself," said Chris with a shrug. "The point is, I traded a little information with your father. I told him we had seen the ghost, and he told us why. If that wasn't a fair trade, I don't know what is."

I was trying to come up with an answer to this when the silver BMW pulled up to the curb and Melissa stepped out.

"Watch this," Chris whispered.

"Hello, troops," said Melissa, walking over to us. "You can stop worrying. The star has arrived."

"What a relief," said Chris sarcastically. Then, before Melissa could respond, she asked, "Did you ever see the ghost, Melissa?"

Melissa looked at her in disgust. "What do you think I am?" she snapped. "Crazy?"

Chris winked at me, and I realized the trap she had set for Melissa.

"That's amazing," said Chris, her eyes wide and innocent. "According to the legend, the ghost only appears to young women who truly love the theater. So I was sure you would have seen her."

My snort of laughter was cut off by a familiar scream.

"Lydia again!" said Chris grimly. "Let's see what's bothering her this time."

Working together, we managed to beat Melissa to the door. Lydia was standing in the center of the lobby, clutching shredded white fabric in her hands.

"It was her!" she screamed. "She did this. She's out to get me! I tell you, the Woman in White is out to get me!"

"Lydia, for heaven's sake, calm down," said Edgar, who was standing in front of her with his clipboard in his hand. "What are you babbling about, anyway?"

"Babbling?" screamed Lydia as she shook out the bundle of fabric. "You call this babbling?"

Without intending to, I gasped. It was the beautiful gown she herself had chosen to wear at the end of Act One.

It had been torn to pieces.

As I watched the blood drain from Edgar's face, I could feel Chris's fingers digging into my arm.

"What is going on in this theater?" she whispered.

CHAPTER EIGHT

The Crowd Goes Nuts

The theater was in an uproar. A couple of women from the chorus had spotted Lydia heading for the lobby with her tattered dress and tagged along to see what was going on. Once they heard what had happened, they started running around, spreading the word that the ghost was getting violent. It didn't take long until the entire cast was in a frenzy. People were demanding protection and wanting to know what the theater was going to do about the ghost. Half a dozen people announced they were going to quit the show. A couple of the women were crying. It didn't look like things were going to quiet down any time soon.

Gwendolyn Meyer did a good imitation of a bull elephant as she herded the entire cast into the first two rows of the theater. Except Lydia, of course. Gwendolyn gave Ken Abbott the key to her office and asked him to take Lydia there so she could lie down until she recovered.

Chris, Melissa, and I ended up sitting in the center of the second row. Somehow, Chris managed to maneuver things so I was sitting next to Melissa. I wish I could figure out how she did it!

Once everyone else was seated, Gwendolyn, Edgar, and the rest of the production crew lined themselves up along the edge of the stage to quiet us down. To me it was like trying to put out a forest fire by spitting on it. But little by little people became quiet and ready to listen to what was being said.

Gwendolyn spoke first. "You people are acting like complete imbeciles, and I think it's time you stopped."

It wasn't really the best way to calm everyone down. We all began muttering angrily.

Edgar rose to the occasion. Putting a hand on Gwendolyn's arm to warn her to back off, he said loudly, "Listen, people. I know a couple of strange things have happened in the last few days. But I'm afraid you're letting your imaginations run away with you."

There it was—the dreaded phrase. That was one of the reasons I hadn't wanted to tell anybody about seeing the ghost to begin with. I knew I would hear: "Your imagination is running away with you." It's one of my least favorite sentences in the whole world.

"Now, let's think about this rationally," said Edgar, slowly walking down a set of stairs on the side of the stage. He walked over to the front row and began to stride back and forth just in front of it. "What's really happened here? Lydia claims to have seen the ghost. And her dress has been cut up. What does all this mean?"

"It means this place has one cranky ghost," said Ken Abbott, returning to the theater and sliding into a seat just ahead of us. This got a couple of nervous laughs and a few angry mutters.

"Does it really?" asked Edgar sharply. "Or does it mean we've got a group of imaginative people doing a play about a woman who met a tragic death—and doing it in the very theater where she died. A theater where her ghost—it has been rumored—has been appearing for fifty years. Under the circumstances, it makes sense for poor Lydia to get spooked occasionally. In fact, I might be worried about how seriously she was taking her part if she didn't. But that doesn't mean the place is haunted."

"What about the dress?" Marilyn Williams asked. Marilyn was a very pretty actress who was playing the part of Lily Larkin's best friend.

"Well, let's think about the dress," said Edgar. "Obviously there's something strange going on. But how strange? Again, let's think carefully. This theater is open all day long. We're located on a busy downtown street where a lot of crazies hang out. A dress is torn up. Does it really make sense to think it was done by a ghost? Or is it more likely that it was one of our local looney birds?"

Paula coughed, and suddenly Edgar began to blush and stammer. He got control of himself quickly, but it was clear something had upset him.

Chris leaned over to me and whispered, "What was that all about?"

"I don't know," I hissed back. "But it was definitely weird. I'd like—"

I was interrupted by Mark Jordan, one of our dancers. "Then you're saying this theater isn't haunted?"

"I'm saying so what if it is?" said Edgar. "People have been saying the place is haunted for nearly fifty years now, and in all that time the ghost hasn't done one bit of harm. Why should she start now?"

"Maybe she doesn't like the script," Ken Abbott said.

"Thanks a lot, Ken," said Alan Bland.

"Hey," Paula said. "It's an old theatrical tradition. When something goes wrong, blame the writer!"

"That's what Lydia said," chimed in Marilyn. "Well, I mean, she didn't say she doesn't like the script. But she told me she thinks the ghost might not want us to do the play."

"Or maybe Marilyn doesn't want Lydia to do the part," hissed Melissa smugly. I looked at her. "Well, after all," she whispered, "if Lydia drops out, Marilyn would get her part."

Leave it to Melissa to think of something like that. The idea probably came naturally to her. I wouldn't have been surprised if it was the sort of thing she might do herself. Personally, I thought Marilyn was kind of nice. It had never occurred to me she might want Lydia out of the way so she could have her role.

But now that the idea had been planted in my mind, it made a certain amount of sense. I wished Melissa had been sitting somewhere else—like Mars, for instance. I don't like thinking about people that way.

"I just want to know one thing," said Sandy Patterson, one of the girls in the chorus. "Is this theater haunted, or isn't it?"

For a moment nobody said anything. I don't know what was going on in other people's minds, but I was engaged in a full-scale argument with myself about whether or not to speak up and admit I had seen the ghost.

She asked a question, said one part of me. *Answer it!*

Don't be stupid! said another. *She didn't ask you. She asked the people in charge. Let them answer.*

"Of course it's haunted," said Gwendolyn. "It's haunted by the memory of every actor who has ever worked here, and every show that's ever been put on here. It's haunted by nearly sixty years of everything that happens in a theater, all the love and hate and anger and tears that go into making a show.

"It's haunted by applause, and the memory of greatness. It's haunted by the things that haunt every theater worth working in, and if you want to keep working on stage, you'd better get used to them."

Well, all in all, it was one of the best speeches I'd ever heard. Gwendolyn talked about theatrical traditions, and the show must go on, and what's a little ghost compared to being on the stage, and not confusing facts with fears, and all kinds of other stuff. I thought it was really impressive. At least, it convinced me. I was ready to jump up on the stage and start acting that very minute.

"What a performance," said Melissa after Gwendolyn was all done.

I looked at her strangely.

"Oh, come on," she said. "It was a terrific speech. But don't get all dreamy eyed about it. What you just saw was acting, pure and simple."

As much as it galled me to agree with Melissa, I had to admit she was right. It was a remarkably good piece of acting.

But somehow the way Melissa said it made it sound as though there was something wrong with that. I felt confused. If someone else had given Gwendolyn's speech, it probably wouldn't have worked half so well. Did that mean there was something wrong with the speech? Was it wrong for Gwendolyn to use her skills to persuade us?

I was trying to figure all that out when two things happened. One: Barney Caulfield got in a shouting match with Gwendolyn. Two: I felt a cold chill run down my spine.

The first was easy to explain. Despite Gwendolyn's speech, Barney started asking stupid questions and talking about walking out on the show. Gwendolyn, who had been quiet and reasonable for more than ten minutes that night—which was about her limit—went off like a skyrocket. It was no big surprise.

The chill down my spine was a little more difficult to explain—until I turned around and saw the Woman in White sitting in the seat behind me. She seemed to be listening to Gwendolyn and Barney argue.

She had a sad look on her face. But she was beautiful. Really, truly beautiful.

I gave Chris a little nudge with my elbow. She turned to see what I wanted and caught her breath.

"It's her!" she whispered.

The Woman in White gave us a tiny smile. Then she raised a finger to her lips, indicating that we should keep quiet.

Unfortunately, Melissa noticed that we weren't paying any attention to the Barney-Gwendolyn argument. "What are you two looking at?" she asked loudly. "The ghost?"

Chris started to laugh. "I knew she couldn't see her," she said.

"You *are* looking at the ghost!" yelped Melissa.

That was all it took. The Woman in White faded out of sight.

And the crowd went nuts.

CHAPTER NINE

Gwendolyn

As things worked out, we had no rehearsal that night. When the excitement finally died down, Gwendolyn just sent the cast home. I assumed she was hoping that by morning we would settle down—and that by the next night most of us would be back, ready to work.

Actually, she didn't dismiss quite everyone. Chris, Melissa, and I were taken to her office for special treatment.

She was furious, of course. That didn't really bother me that much: Gwendolyn was always furious. But Edgar was with her, and the look in his eyes was breaking my heart. I could tell he thought we had started all that trouble just trying to be funny. As far as he was concerned, we had stabbed him in the back. It was killing me to have him believe that.

I don't think there's any feeling in the world worse than having someone you care about think you've let them down.

Gwendolyn started things off. "I cannot accept such foolish, irresponsible, stupid, childish behavior in this theater. That little stunt you three pulled tonight was one of the most unwarranted, unkind . . ."

Well, you get the idea. She was off and running, and it was several minutes before she managed to wind down.

"Now, do you have anything to say for yourselves?" she asked at last, glaring at us as if the first person who actually did say anything would immediately be torn to pieces.

"Yes," said Chris. "We do."

I kicked her. Hadn't she learned there were times when it's safer to keep your mouth shut, even if you're in the right?

"Well?" said Gwendolyn, drawing out the word very slowly. It was the most dangerous sounding "well" I had ever heard.

I had to admire Chris. Other than a tiny tremble in her voice, which you might not have noticed if you weren't used to the way she talked, she didn't show any sign of backing down. She was braver than I would have been in her shoes!

"We weren't fooling around," said Chris. "The ghost *was* sitting right behind us."

Gwendolyn looked at Chris shrewdly. Without saying a word, she turned her attention to Melissa. "Did you see the ghost?" she asked.

I bit the corners of my mouth to keep from smiling. If Melissa lied and said she had, which seemed to me perfectly likely, there was no telling what Gwendolyn might do to her.

But if she told the truth, she would be admitting to Chris and me that she didn't love the theater enough for the Woman in White to appear to her. I could almost hear the wheels turning in her head while she tried to figure out what to say. It reminded me of something my mother used to tell me when I was little: "One nice thing about the truth is it's usually less work."

"Well?" asked Gwendolyn when Melissa didn't answer for a long time.

Melissa finally decided to tell the truth. "No, Mrs. Meyer, I didn't see the ghost." If you want my opinion, she didn't tell the truth for any moral reason. It was just that she had decided Chris was bluffing.

Gwendolyn stared at Melissa for a moment but didn't say anything else. Then she turned her attention to me. Narrowing her eyes, she asked, "And what about you, Nine?"

Well, what was I going to do? I knew Chris would never leave *me* hanging. So even though my stomach was turning flip-flops, I nodded my head, took a deep breath, and said, "I saw her."

Gwendolyn got this incredibly strange look on her face.

"Describe her to me," she said to Chris.

I was puzzled. If Gwendolyn didn't believe in the ghost, what difference did it make what we thought she looked like? It wasn't like that morning when I was testing Chris by checking her description against the script.

Or at least, it didn't seem that way. But as Chris described the ghost, the expression on Gwendolyn's face began to soften. "That's right," she said, nodding her head in satisfaction. "That's right."

I looked at her in astonishment.

"That's just the way it was when I saw her," she said.

All three of us started to talk at once. Gwendolyn cut us off by simply talking louder than the three of us put together.

"Oh, don't look so surprised," she snapped. "Of course I've seen the ghost. It was quite awhile ago, naturally. You do know the story, don't you? That she only appears to young women who love the theater. In fact, I'm surprised you haven't seen her, Melissa."

I bit my cheeks so I wouldn't laugh. My opinion of Gwendolyn was flipping back and forth so fast I couldn't keep track of it. I was angry that she had lied to the rest of the cast when she told them the theater wasn't haunted. But I could have hugged her for the little zinger she had just given Melissa.

"Anyway," said Gwendolyn, "it's been more than a little while since I qualified as a young woman. But I saw her in my day. Oh, yes, indeed. I did see her."

She seemed to drift off for a moment.

Edgar was looking at the four of us as if we were all from another planet.

"Why didn't you say something back in the theater?" Chris asked Gwendolyn.

"Be sensible," she answered. "Can you imagine the effect that would have had on those ninnies? You know what they say about freedom of speech: It doesn't extend to shouting 'Fire!' in a crowded theater. My saying I've seen the ghost would have been the same thing."

"But it's not the same," I protested. "Of course you're not supposed to shout 'Fire' if there isn't one. But there really was a fire—or ghost—in this case."

The second I finished, I could have bitten my tongue. I had gotten so wrapped up in the conversation I forgot it was *Gwendolyn* I was talking to. I winced and waited for her to start yelling.

"Good point, Nine," she said in a totally reasonable tone of voice. "Maybe I was mistaken."

Sometimes I think that was the biggest surprise of that entire surprising night.

Chris said the same thing after we left. Actually, her exact words were, "I almost fell off my chair when the old bat admitted she was wrong." But you get the idea.

We were feeling pretty good, despite the fact that Melissa was still with us. Once Gwendolyn was convinced we had actually seen the ghost, she was a lot less angry about the fuss we had caused. She did ask us to try to keep our mouths shut about the whole thing, since the cast was panicked enough already.

When I had asked her about Lydia's dress she got a concerned look on her face. "I don't know what that was all about," she had said firmly. "But I do know the ghost of Lily Larkin didn't do that damage."

I was going to bring the question up to Chris as we were walking through the lobby, but she spoke first.

"Let's cut through the theater," she said. "My father said he wants to pick me up on Jefferson Street from now on, because the traffic's not so tricky. The side exit will take us out right where he wants to meet us."

"Won't it be locked?" I asked.

"Nah, Pop won't be locking up for an hour or two yet. Come on."

"Well, *my* father is picking me up out front," said Melissa, as if that were somehow more respectable. She flounced off through the lobby.

"Come on," said Chris, taking me by the arm. I wasn't really sure I wanted to go back into the theater. But since I was riding home with Chris, I didn't have much choice.

Besides, I had a feeling I knew what was really going through her mind when she suggested the detour: she was hoping we might have a chance to see the ghost again. I could tell she was beginning to feel the way I did about the ghost, that she was almost like a friend.

We pulled open the big brass and glass doors and stepped into the theater. It seemed much spookier than earlier in the evening, when everyone else had been in it. A single worklight was burning on the stage. Other than that it was dark. Very dark.

"Let's go out the front way," I said nervously.

"Don't be a wimp," whispered Chris. "Come on!"

"Why are we speaking in whispers?" I asked—speaking in a whisper myself.

Chris shrugged. I knew what she meant. There wasn't any logical reason. It just seemed the right thing to do.

We began tiptoeing down the aisle. Suddenly Chris put her hand on my arm. "What's that?" she hissed.

I stopped dead in my tracks. It took a moment for me to locate the sound. Finally I realized it was coming from the front of the theater.

But it wasn't the ghost. It was Pop. He was sitting in the third row, crying his eyes out.

CHAPTER TEN

More Costumes

It was almost eleven by the time Chris and her father dropped me off. I found my dad in the kitchen, stirring something in a big bowl.

"Hi, babe," he said cheerfully as I walked in. "How'd rehearsal go?"

"Don't ask," I sighed, poking my finger into the bowl. I took out a glob of something kind of purple and stuck it in my mouth. "Not bad," I said. "What is it?"

"Slopnuggets."

Slopnuggets are my father's own invention. They're something he came up with after my mother left. Basically, he takes the biggest bowl he can find and throws in anything he thinks might make a good cookie that night. Then he stirs it all up and bakes it. They never come out the same twice, but he's never made a batch I didn't like, either. He claims the trick is to avoid things like pickles and sauerkraut. Sometimes we make them together. It can get a little hysterical when we do.

My father knew that I knew he was making slopnuggets. What I really wanted to know was what made them purple. I raised an eyebrow and stared at him.

"The secret ingredient of the night is black raspberry Jell-O," he said, without my having to ask again. "Except now it's not a secret anymore. So much for surprises. Anyway, I repeat—but only because you told me not to, so I'm assuming it must be really interesting—how did rehearsal go tonight?"

"Well, somebody tore Lydia's main costume to shreds; the whole cast got scared because they thought the ghost did it; Gwendolyn had a screaming fit; and Chris and I almost caused a panic in the theater when the ghost sat down behind us."

"You're right," he said, dumping some baking soda into the bowl. "I shouldn't have asked. But since we've gone this far, you have to tell me what happened next. I'm fascinated."

So I told him about the meeting in Gwendolyn's office and about how we had decided to walk out through the theater when it was over. I told him about hearing Pop crying.

"What did you do?" he asked.

"We turned around and went out the other way. I don't think he even knew we were there. I figured he wanted to be alone."

"Good move," my dad said, shoving Sidney out of the way with his foot so he could get a cookie sheet out of the cupboard. "What are you going to do next?"

"Go to bed!" I said, trying to keep down a yawn. "I'm exhausted."

"That's two good moves," he said. "Then what?"

"I'm going to get up."

"And then?" he persisted.

"And then I'm going to find out what's going on in that theater!" I said emphatically.

He nodded. "That's what I figured."

"You don't mind?" I asked cautiously.

"Of course I mind!" he said. "You're probably going to get in as much trouble as people usually do when they stick their noses in other people's business, though I suppose I should be used to that by now. The real reason I mind is that I'm jealous."

"Jealous?"

"Sure. I've never even seen a ghost. But if this one keeps appearing to you, odds are she wants your help for some reason. I suppose you'd better give it to her."

I still don't know if he really meant that, or if he said it just to scare me.

"Scare you," said Chris the next day when I met her at the theater. "Definitely. But not enough to get you to leave things alone. Just enough to get you to be careful. Your father is incredibly cool. You want to trade?"

"Not really," I said. "Losing one parent was enough to last me forever."

"Divorce?" asked Chris sympathetically.

I shrugged. "Not yet. But they've been separated for two years."

Chris shook her head. "I'm sorry," she said. "Want to talk about it?"

"No. At least, not right now."

Chris didn't push. I knew she wouldn't. "Some other time," she said. "We've got work to do anyway. Let's get busy."

We began walking toward the theater, which was one long block up from where the bus let me off. We hadn't gone more than halfway when Chris grabbed my arm and dragged me into a store entryway.

I was getting better at this detective business. I managed to beat down my first reaction, which was to yell, "What do you think you're doing?" and replace it with a very quietly hissed, "What's up?"

"Look down there," said Chris, gesturing with her thumb.

Poking my head around the corner of the entryway, I spotted Alan Bland and Lydia Crane stepping into a restaurant called the Brass Elephant, which was a hangout for most of the adult members of the cast. Lydia was holding Alan's arm and leaning against him in a very possessive way.

"Are they going out?" Chris asked gleefully.

"I don't know," I said. "Alan's a nice guy. But he doesn't seem like the type a beautiful woman like Lydia would be interested in."

Chris shrugged. "Some women just go nuts for skinny intellectuals."

I wondered if Chris was trying to tease me about my crush on Edgar. He could certainly be classified as a skinny intellectual, even if he was about ten times as gorgeous as Alan.

We had to walk past the Brass Elephant to get to the theater, and we wanted to look inside without making it seem obvious. We decided that just as we reached the restaurant's window, I would bend down to tie the laces of my sneakers. As I bent over, Chris stood there tapping her foot impatiently, just as we had planned. I took enough time doing my laces for her to get a good look through the window.

"Well?" I asked, when I was ready to move on. "Could you see them?"

"Could I ever," said Chris. "They were sitting in a little booth near the front, with their hands on the table and their fingertips *almost* touching. I couldn't see Alan's face, but Lydia was looking at him like she thought he was wonderful. A real romance! I love it."

"If that's a romance, I'll eat my sneakers," I said, as we walked through the big front doors of the theater. I looked up at the giant mural on the wall and touched the brass elephant, just as I always did. The place seemed so bright and cheerful in the daytime it was hard to believe such strange things were going on at night.

"Well, where do we start?" said Chris.

Before I could answer, Eileen Taggart, the costume designer, swooped down on us. "Just the two I wanted to see!" she shrieked joyfully. "I can't believe you're here just when I need you."

"It's a knack we have," said Chris dryly as Eileen led us off to her fitting room at the back of the theater. There she stood me up on a hassock and started trying different ratty old dresses on me, babbling along merrily as she did.

"You're awfully cheerful today," said Chris. "Aren't you upset about Lydia's costume? It must have been an awful lot of work for you."

"Not hardly!" said Eileen, jabbing a pin through several layers of fabric. "It was something they had hanging around from a show they did three years ago. I hated the thing myself. I kept telling Gwendolyn that if she let Lydia wear it in the show I wasn't going to have my name on the program! Oh, dear, this looks like poop, don't it, love," she added, tearing off the last skirt she had wrapped around me.

I glanced at Chris, who nodded her head in response. All of a sudden we had someone with a motive for destroying the costume!

Eileen chattered on, totally unaware of what we were thinking. "'Course, I don't know why I'm doing this show, anyway," she said as she dove into a box filled with stuff that looked like it had been rejected by the Salvation Army. "I told Edgar I didn't think he ought to do a show by a looney bird."

She gasped and put her hand to her mouth. "I wasn't supposed to say anything about that. Oh, well, it's no big secret anyhow."

"What isn't?" asked Chris innocently.

"Oh, about that Alan Bland," replied Eileen, perfectly happy to spread some gossip. "They packed him away for a few months last year, you know. Nutty as a fruitcake, though you wouldn't know it to look at him now. Not that he's normal, or anything. But he doesn't give you the idea that there are little bats flying around in his head anymore, if you know what I mean."

I could feel my mind spinning. If Alan Bland had mental problems, was it possible he was crazy enough to be sabotaging his own show? It didn't seem logical. But then, crazy people aren't supposed to be logical. Anyway, now we had to add Alan to our list of suspects.

"Oscar Hammerstein spent some time in a mental hospital, once," said Chris. "You know, the guy from Rodgers and Hammerstein. He wrote some of his best stuff after he came out."

"You don't say!" shrieked Eileen happily as she tore the sleeve off an old blouse. "Here, this might work for your first scene in Act One, love," she said, fitting it on me. After a few pokes and pulls, she said, "Jump down now, that's a good girl. And you hop up, Miss Chris."

Chris looked at me helplessly. It was clear that Eileen had totally missed her point about Alan. I shrugged. I figured we might as well let Eileen babble on and see if we could learn anything else.

The plan worked halfway: she kept babbling, but we didn't learn anything more worth knowing.

"Even so, it was worth it," Chris said as we walked away from the costume room. "We did pick up a couple of suspects. Plus we had our first costume fittings. Which puts us ahead of most of the cast."

"How did you know that thing about Oscar Hammerstein?" I asked. "Or did you just make it up?"

"No, it's real. My father's a big musical theater fan. He knows all that kind of stuff. You can't shut him up about it. It rubs off, I guess. I probably wouldn't—"

I never did find out what Chris probably wouldn't, because Pop came walking past us right then. Chris stopped talking and jabbed me in the ribs with her elbow. "Let's follow him," she whispered. "He's a suspicious character if I ever saw one."

I hesitated. We were on shaky ground being in the building as it was. I didn't think Pop would take kindly to it if he spotted us tailing him. "Oh, why bother," I said. "He's just an unhappy old man. How many secrets can he have?"

While we were trying to decide whether or not to follow Pop, a familiar voice called my name. "Nine! Come here, will you? I need to talk to you."

CHAPTER ELEVEN

One of the Ten Stupidest Things I've Ever Done

It was Paula Geller. She was standing on the stage with a stack of music clutched in her arms. Her red hair was pulled back in a tight braid that dangled over one shoulder.

"I never knew this place was so busy during the daytime," whispered Chris as we walked down the aisle to join Paula at the front of the theater.

"I'm glad I spotted you, Nine," said Paula, as we climbed the steps at the side of the stage. "I've been working on your solo, and I think I've taken care of that spot where you were having trouble."

"You changed the music?" I gasped.

"Sure," said Paula. "Why not?"

"But that was the way the song was *supposed* to be. You can't go changing it just because I couldn't sing it."

Paula looked at me strangely. "Nine, who wrote the song?"

"I thought you did," I answered.

"Well, there you are. If I can write it, I can rewrite it. It's not like it's an old standard. Alan and I are still working on it."

"You change stuff after it's all written?" I asked.

Paula burst out laughing. "If you want it to be any good you do," she said. "Haven't you ever heard of second drafts? Or fifteenth drafts? I get the feeling you're worried that I'm going to ruin my song just so you can sing it."

I nodded my head.

"Well, get rid of that idea right now," said Paula firmly. "Songs are just like stories and poems. They aren't written so much as rewritten."

That made about as much sense as saying "black is white," and I said so. Actually, I didn't put

it quite that way. I think my exact word was
"Huh?"

"You act like writing is something magical,"
said Paula. "As if things always came out right the
first time."

"Don't they?"

"My poor little Nine," said Paula. "I hope
you're planning to be something simple when you
grow up. Like a tax lawyer. Every once in a while a
song comes out right the first time. And those
times *are* magical. But mostly it's just hard work—
writing it over and over until you get it as good as
you can. Sometimes a song doesn't work at all.
Alan and I threw out more songs than we kept
while we were writing the show."

I couldn't believe such waste. "You guys are
crazy!" I said.

Did you ever wish you could take your tongue
and tie it in a knot so it would stop getting you in
trouble? As soon as the words were out of my
mouth, I remembered what Eileen had just told us
about Alan. Actually, I probably would have been
all right even then if I could have just let things
alone. But not me. No. What did I do? I clapped my
hands over my mouth and looked horrified. "Like a
complete idiot" was the way Chris described it
later. She was right.

Paula looked at me sharply. "I take it you've
heard about Alan's problem," she said softly.

I was so embarrassed I think my toes were blushing. I nodded my head, afraid that if I opened my mouth I might say something stupid again.

Paula sighed. "Come with me. I want to have a talk with the two of you."

Half an hour later I knew more than I ever wanted to know about mental illness. I also knew a lot about Alan Bland and how brave he was. That was the main thing that came through in Paula's talk with us. How much courage it had taken for Alan to put his life back together after things had gone haywire.

By the time she was done, I was pretty much convinced that Alan Bland would not try to wreck his own show.

Not only that, I could sing my song! It turned out that half the problem had been the song and half had been my nervousness, which was largely because of Melissa's judging me.

"Now, think for a minute," said Paula. "If having Melissa watch you makes you so nervous you can't sing, what do you think it does to Alan to know people are watching him for any little sign that he's going to mess up his whole life?"

I thought about it. I didn't like it. "Should we say something to him?"

"Yeah. 'Hi. How are you? I like the show. I don't like the show.' The same kind of stuff you'd say to anybody. Don't treat him like he's different or anything. Here, hit this note."

I did. It sounded wonderful, if I do say so myself.

"Perfect. Now scram, you guys. I've got work to do."

Chris and I didn't have to be told twice. We scooted out of Paula's practice room and back down the stairs toward the lobby. We had a lot more investigating to do before the day was over!

We had almost made it to the stairway when a brassy voice called out, "What are you two doing here?"

Gwendolyn! I couldn't believe it. Didn't the people in that theater have anything better to do than hang around and look for kids they could bother?

"We've been working with Paula," said Chris quite honestly. "Just wait till you hear Nine's song! By the way, do you know where Pop is?"

I wished I could be cool like that. It was unbelievable. Chris stood right in front of Stone-face Gwendolyn Meyer and without blinking an eye convinced her to tell us what we wanted to know.

Gwendolyn told us we would probably find Pop in the theater and also told us where his office was, in case we had to leave him a message.

We headed for the theater. Sure enough, there was Pop, fixing a broken seat near the back.

Suddenly it hit me that I had no idea what to do next. "What are we going to say to him?" I whispered to Chris.

"Nothing, dummy. We don't want to talk to him at all. We're heading for his office."

That didn't stop her from waving and shouting a cheerful "Hi, Pop!" as we went strolling by. Pop looked up from the seat he was working on, scowled at us, and made a noise that may or may not have been a greeting. We continued on down the center aisle as if we owned the place.

Behind the stage was the stairway that led up to the dressing rooms. There was also a down stairway. That was where Gwendolyn had told us we would find Pop's office.

We stood at the top of the stairs and looked down. Neither of us moved. I had a feeling we were each waiting for the other to go first.

"Dark down there," said Chris after a while.

"Sure is," I said. I was squinting down the steps, trying to make something out.

"Person might get hurt, stumbling around."

"Sure could," I said.

"They ought to keep it better lit."

"Sure should," I said, getting ready to turn around and leave.

"Well, let's get on with it," said Chris. She started walking down the stairs.

I couldn't believe it! I thought she had been trying to talk herself out of going down there. The truth was, she had just been building up her courage.

Now I had to build up mine!

It helped to have Chris ahead of me. I started after her, sticking as close to her as I could.

When we reached the bottom of the stairs, we were standing in a little hall. A large space opened off to the right. It wasn't as dark as I had thought, because a few dim lights were on. We could see, but the lights also threw weird shadows all over the walls.

It would have been spooky under the best of conditions. Knowing there was a ghost hanging around made it worse. It didn't make any difference that I was convinced the ghost was friendly. The hairs on the back of my neck were slowly starting to stand up. I shook my head and shivered as a chill ran down my spine.

We walked along the hall to the larger room. The concrete walls were damp and cool to the touch even though it was summer.

The place was littered with old props and pieces of scenery. Seen up close, a lot of the ones that were supposed to be scary were kind of funny.

But some of the funny ones were downright terrifying.

There was one that I still see in my nightmares sometimes—a gigantic clown face that had been propped up against the far wall. It had to have been at least ten feet tall. I don't have any idea what they used it for originally, but I imagined it looked wonderful and jolly when it was on the stage.

But now it was standing in front of a light fixture, so light streamed out of its eyes and mouth. It looked evil. I stood in front of it for the longest time, fascinated by it, yet afraid at the same time.

I rubbed my arms as if I were freezing and tried to turn away. But it was as though I were under a spell. I didn't seem to be able to take my attention off the clown face until Chris called my name.

"Hey, Nine!" she said. "Look at this!"

I turned around and saw her sitting in a fake coffin held up by a pair of sawhorses. I wondered where it had come from. Then I remembered that the day of the auditions my father had mentioned seeing a stage version of *Dracula* here a few years ago.

"I'm looking for blood donors," said Chris. "Anyone want to volunteer?"

I laughed in spite of myself. "Chris, get out of that thing before someone catches us down here!"

"I can't! I'm one of the living dead! Watch!"

With that, she lay back in the coffin and pulled the lid completely shut.

"Chris!"

Slowly the lid of the coffin began to rise again.

I thought I was going to go out of my skin. I mean, I knew who it was and what was going on. But being down there with all that weird stuff was making me pretty jumpy.

Suddenly Chris sat straight up in the coffin, crossed her eyes, and stuck her front teeth out over her lower lip. "Where's that beautiful Edgar?" she cried. "I want to bite his neck!"

"Chris!"

"OK, OK," she said, climbing out of the coffin. "Here, you try it."

"Are you crazy?"

"No! Come on. You may never have a chance like this again."

Even now I can't believe I was stupid enough to let her talk me into it. But I climbed into the coffin to see what it felt like.

I had to admit, it was an interesting experience. I mean, did you ever get to sit in a coffin?

"Now close the lid," Chris said.

"Are you crazy?" I said for about the fifteenth time.

"Come on, Nine. You won't know how weird it is unless you close the lid. Besides, I want to see what it looks like when you open it. You got to see me do it. I bet it was really creepy. I want to see it, too."

"Oh, OK," I said grumpily.

"Great!" said Chris, stepping away from the coffin.

Feeling foolish, I took hold of the handle inside the lid and lay back. (Yes, I know. Coffins don't usually have handles inside their lids. But this one was made especially for a show, remember?)

As I brought the lid down over my face, I tried to imagine it really was closing on me for the last time. I figured as long as I was at it, I might as well go for the whole experience.

It spooked me for a minute. But once I got over my initial scare, it was so dark and quiet and cozy I almost decided I liked it.

I took a moment to figure out what I would say when I opened the lid. I can't remember the line now, but I thought it was really funny at the time.

Unfortunately, when I pushed on the lid to get out, it wouldn't budge.

CHAPTER TWELVE

Headline News

I pushed again. Nothing.

"Chris!" I yelled. "Quit fooling around! Let me out of here!"

"Well, open the lid and get out," said Chris. "I'm not stopping you."

If I live to be a hundred, I doubt that moment will ever come off my list of the ten worst things that ever happened to me.

I smashed my hands against the lid of the coffin. "CHRIS!" I screamed. "GET ME OUT OF HERE!"

"Hold still!" yelled Chris. "I'm trying!"

I could hear her scratching and poking around the edges of the lid.

I took a deep breath and tried to hold still. That got me to wondering if there were air holes in the coffin. Weird visions began to flash through my head. I saw my entire fifth-grade class coming to my funeral. I saw our teacher, Mrs. Grambicki, standing at the edge of the coffin, dabbing her eyes with a handkerchief and talking about what a good kid I had been.

"It won't budge!" Chris said, interrupting my funeral. "I think it's broken."

I think I went a little crazy right then. I remember pounding against the lid like a little kid having a tantrum.

"Hold still!" Chris yelled. "You'll knock the thing off the sawhorses. You might break it."

"I don't care if it breaks!" I yelled. "Get me out of here!"

Chris started to say something, but she was interrupted by an angry voice yelling about "all the racket going on down there!"

It was Pop.

I stopped pounding. I knew Pop would get me out of the coffin. But I had a feeling when he did I might wish I was back inside it again.

The next few minutes were a jumble of voices and noises. Pop yelled at Chris about the trouble she was causing, and Chris yelled right back, trying to explain to him about my being trapped in the coffin.

Finally it dawned on him what she was saying. "Damn fool kids," he muttered. He began banging at the side of the coffin. Suddenly the bottom opened up, and I came crashing down onto the floor.

"Ouch!" I yelped. "That hurt!"

"Serves you right!" said Pop gruffly. "The two of you don't have any business fooling around down here, anyway. Let me see your hands," he added.

At first I didn't know what he was talking about. Then I realized that he had noticed what I hadn't even felt in all the excitement: my hands were scraped and bleeding from pounding on the lid of the coffin.

I held them out for his inspection. He grabbed them, turned them over roughly, then said, "We'd better take care of these. Come with me."

Glancing at each other nervously, Chris and I followed Pop to his office, which was where we had been trying to go before we got distracted by all those props. Only we had intended to go in without Pop, so we could check things out.

Actually, I'm not sure "office" is the right word for the place. It was just a large, dingy room filled almost to overflowing with stuff most people would consider junk. A big old wooden desk stood to the right of the door, and a cluttered table stretched along the left wall. At the back of the room was another door, pulled nearly shut.

Personally, I thought it was wonderful. Most of the stuff that looked like junk was really souvenirs from all of Pop's years at the theater: posters, playbills, tattered scripts—all kinds of stuff. And the new stuff was all from the theater, too. I recognized a couple of props I knew we would be using in our show. It was clear they were only half-finished, and it dawned on me that Pop must be working on them.

But the most amazing things had to be the pictures. A few dozen of them hung on the rear wall, mounted in cheap black wooden frames. The glass had cracked in three or four of them, and a few had started to fade. Even so, they were impressive. They were all pictures of important stars—people I recognized immediately from all the old movies I had watched with my father. And every one of them was autographed.

I was dying to go over and look at them more closely. But the way Pop said, "Sit here," when he plunked me down in the chair beside his desk made me change my mind.

So I sat and glared at Chris as she casually wandered over to the wall and began to inspect the pictures.

Pop sat down at his desk and began rummaging through the drawers. As he did I looked over the rest of the room. I was surprised to see what looked like a bed in the next room.

Did Pop live in the theater?

I made up my mind to ask around and see what I could find out.

"Here, give me your hands," said Pop. He was holding a tube of some kind of salve he had pulled out of one of the drawers.

I stuck out my hands and let him start rubbing on the salve. As he did, I noticed a large scrapbook sitting on the far side of the desk.

It was open to a page that contained a single sheet of yellowed newspaper. It was upside down, but even from where I was sitting I could make out the huge black headline: "ACTRESS KILLED IN TRAGIC ACCIDENT AT GRAND THEATER."

It was the article we had been trying to find in the library!

Underneath the headline there was a sub-head. Because it was upside down and smaller than the headline, it was hard to make out. Squinting a bit, I leaned toward the scrapbook and let out a little gasp as the words came together for me. They were simple but shocking: "Andrew Heron Accused in Love Triangle Murder."

Pop heard my gasp. Realizing what I was looking at, he reached out and closed the scrap-book.

"You know what smart kids do?" he asked.

My eyes were wide as I shook my head.

"They keep their mouths shut, and their noses in their own business," said Pop. "This is very good advice. If you have any brains, you'll take it. Understand?"

"Y-yes, sir," I stammered.

"Good," said Pop. "Now, beat it. Both of you!"

He didn't have to tell me twice. Chris, un-aware of what I had just seen, didn't want to leave. She wanted to ask Pop some questions.

Grabbing her by the arm, I dragged her out of Pop's office and up the stairs.

CHAPTER THIRTEEN

Dropouts

"Well, it's Pop," said Chris as we were riding the bus home. "He killed Lily Larkin fifty years ago, and now he's worried that the play is going to stir up all the dirt all over again. Maybe he got away before, and now he's afraid we'll find out he's really Andrew Heron and he'll get slapped in jail."

"Slow down, will you?" I said. "All I saw was a clipping from a newspaper, and you've got the guy convicted already. If he really was Andrew Heron, why would he be hanging around the theater?"

"Guilt," said Chris as if it were the most obvious thing in the world. "The criminal always returns to the scene of the crime."

I snorted. "That's the silliest thing I've ever heard."

"Yeah, well, remember that he was in love with the Woman in White. He probably can't stand to leave the place. He's probably bound to her by some kind of curse."

"Chris, will you start talking sense!"

She gave me a lopsided grin. "Just trying to bug you. I agree, we have to get more evidence. But I still think Pop's the one trying to sabotage the play. He's got to be connected with this thing in some way, or he wouldn't have that clipping."

"Isn't it possible he just has a collection of articles about the theater?" I asked.

"OK," said Chris, falling against me as the bus lurched over a bump, "if it's not Pop, who is it? You got any better candidates?"

"Well, not better. But certainly possible."

"Like who?"

"Like no one. Maybe nobody's really trying to sabotage the play. Maybe Eileen just took advantage of Lydia's nervousness to get rid of that dress she hated. Or maybe Alan Bland has flipped out again and thinks he's the ghost or something. . . ."

It was Chris's turn to protest. "Nine! How can you say that after everything Paula told us today?"

"I'm not saying it's true," I said. "I'm just trying to list all the possibilities."

"Then don't forget Marilyn. She could be trying to drive Lydia out so she gets her part, like Melissa thinks."

"Heck, it could be Melissa," I said.

"Not a chance," said Chris.

"Why not?"

Chris shrugged. "She's not a ghost. She's a witch!"

I was still laughing when we got to Chris's house.

I was also laughing when we left, but that was because I had plenty of fuel in between. Dinner in the Gurley household is hard to describe. The closest I can come is to say it's something like a cross between "Saturday Night Live" and feeding time at the zoo. That's mostly because Chris has a huge batch of brothers. "It's like living with a football team," she complained to me.

It seemed like every brother had something to say about everything that came up. And they all wanted to say it at the same time as loudly as they could. And usually with their mouths full.

No wonder Chris was so tough. She had to be to survive in that household! What a contrast to my own house, where my dad and I sit down to a quiet dinner together every night and just talk about our day.

To tell you the truth, I kind of liked it. At least at Chris's house no one was ever lonely. But then, as my grandmother always said, "If two things are equally pleasant, the one you don't have will always be the one you want." I'd probably have gone crazy if I really had to live at the Gurleys'.

I started to feel a little nervous as Chris's father drove us back to the theater. After everything that had happened there in the last few days, I wondered what would be next. Would there be more trouble? Would the ghost appear again? Would Pop still be mad at us?

But it wasn't just these questions. I also had a *feeling* that something horrible was going to happen. I couldn't have explained it to anyone. It was just something inside me that kept insisting there was real trouble on the way.

It didn't take us long to find out that things had already gone from bad to worse. As we walked into the lobby I spotted Edgar sitting on the broad stairway that led up to the mezzanine. He was clutching his head in his hands. He looked like someone whose dog had just been run over.

Chris and I made sure we took time to pat the brass elephant. Then we walked quietly over to where Edgar sat. Chris plunked herself down on one side of him. I sat on the other.

I felt a warm tingle. This was the closest I had ever gotten to Edgar!

"So," I said. "What's wrong?"

Edgar didn't look up. "Do you want the list in alphabetical or chronological order?"

He sounded so miserable I just wanted to reach out and hug him. But then, I had been wanting to do that since the first time I met him, so I supposed it didn't count for much!

"Let's go for chronological," said Chris. "Mostly because I don't know what it means."

"Time order," said Edgar. "Like this. One o'clock, Billy Klein calls to tell me he's leaving the show. One-fifteen, Lizzie Cramer calls with the same message. A little after two it was Mark Jordan. Ditto."

"Did they say why?" asked Chris.

"Oh, sure, they gave excuses. But the real reason is they're afraid of the ghost."

This seemed so outrageous to me I actually snorted. "What are they scared of?" I asked. "She wouldn't hurt a soul!"

Edgar shook his head. "Not everyone is as trusting as you are, Nine," he said. He stood up. "You two go on in the theater. I have to talk to Gwendolyn for a while."

He started up the stairs, then stopped and looked back at us.

"Thanks for listening," he said. "I appreciate it."

"Whooie," said Chris, after Edgar was gone. "What a mess!"

I nodded in dismal agreement. Mark Jordan was our best dancer. Lizzie Cramer was one of the better singers. And Billy Klein had an important speaking part. All of them gone in a single day, and all because they were afraid of a ghost that wouldn't hurt a fly. No wonder Edgar was depressed!

As for me, I was more determined than ever to get to the bottom of this mess. For one thing, I couldn't stand to see what it was doing to poor Edgar. For another thing, my curiosity was driving me crazy.

Rehearsal started right on time that night. At least everyone who dropped out had called and told Edgar. No one just didn't show up.

Edgar made an announcement that there were going to be some cast changes and that we would try to work around the missing people for a while. He didn't say why the people were gone. But you could tell from the whispers that everyone had guessed.

"OK, Act One, scene four," Edgar said. "I want to change some of the blocking. Melissa, you come up and stand here. Nine, here. And, Chris, over here."

He paced about the stage as he talked, indicating not only where he wanted us to stand but what he wanted us to do while we were there. Soon we were into the scene and working hard. It was fun—about the first real acting I'd done since rehearsals started. Until then Edgar hadn't worked on any of my major scenes; I had spent most of my time working with Paula on my songs.

Unfortunately it was over all too soon, and we went back to our seats while Edgar moved on to the next scene. If there was one thing I learned during rehearsals, it was how much time actors spend sitting around waiting. It could drive a person crazy!

I felt sorry for Edgar as I watched him try to work around the dropouts. It seemed that there wasn't a single scene in the play that didn't use at least one or the other of them.

After about half an hour of reblocking, I felt Chris tap my arm.

When I turned to see what she wanted, she gestured toward the back of the theater. I looked in the direction she was pointing.

The ghost was standing in the aisle, about three rows behind us. When she saw me looking at her, she raised a finger to her lips as if telling me to keep quiet.

Then she held out her hand and crooked a finger. She wanted us to follow her!

I looked at Chris. She looked back and shrugged. Moving as quietly as we could, we slipped out of our seats and followed the ghost up the aisle.

CHAPTER FOURTEEN

Old News

Did you ever watch a ghost walk?

I can't swear they all do it the same way. But it was kind of interesting to watch the Woman in White move up the aisle.

She was wearing the same white dress I always saw her in, which of course was the costume she had been wearing the night she was killed. It was quite a bit nicer than the one Lydia had been supposed to wear. I wasn't surprised that Eileen Taggart had wanted to make something more like the real thing if her name was going to be on the program as costume designer.

Anyway, the gown went down to the floor. As she moved, I had the impression that the Woman in White was actually *walking,* not just gliding along as I would have expected. Dropping back a step, I knelt down and tipped my head sideways so it was right against the floor. I was right—she was moving her feet!

Chris looked back and saw me with my head against the floor.

"What are you doing?" she hissed, grabbing me by the arm and trying to drag me to my feet.

"I'll tell you later," I said. I was busy trying to figure out why a ghost would bother to move her feet when she walked. I thought it must be memory, or habit, or something like that. I couldn't believe they *had to,* especially after we got to the door leading out to the lobby and she walked right through without bothering to open it.

I don't know why it was such a shock to see her do that. I mean, you figure that's the kind of thing a ghost can do. But when I saw her head for the door, walk right up to it, and then *fade through it,* I almost flipped out. I think maybe that was the first time it really sank in that what we were dealing with was an honest-to-goodness ghost. I don't know what I was thinking before that, but suddenly she seemed a lot more real—or unreal. It was freaky.

Chris and I pushed our way through the door. The Woman in White was already halfway across the lobby. She must have figured we were following her because she didn't even look back. Or maybe she had eyes in the back of her head. Who knows what ghosts can do?

She led us up the stairs to the mezzanine area, then through a door that took us into a hallway. After a few minutes I realized she was using a roundabout way to take us to the back of the theater. Before long we were standing at the stairway that led down to the prop and scenery storage area where we had gotten in so much trouble earlier in the day.

I hesitated, but the ghost kept on going, gliding down the stairway like mist along a hillside. Chris grabbed my arm, and down we went.

I figured that the eerie storage room would be less frightening since I already knew what was in it. I was wrong. Somehow knowing that it was nighttime outside made it even worse than it had been before. Or maybe it was the fact that we were sharing the room with a ghost.

The Woman in White led us past the clown face and Dracula's coffin, right to Pop's office. Again, I hung back. I didn't want to get caught snooping around in there!

But she was standing inside waiting for us. In fact, she had an impatient look on her face.

"It's not smart to keep a ghost waiting," Chris said. Grabbing my arm again, she stepped into the office. You may have noticed that Chris was pretty brave—she was always the one to take the first step. But did you also notice that she usually grabbed my arm before she did it?

The ghost was standing beside Pop's desk. The scrapbook we had seen earlier in the day was missing.

She pointed to the middle drawer. I opened it. The scrapbook lay inside.

"I guess she wants us to read it," said Chris.

That made sense to me. I was worried about snooping around in Pop's stuff. But if the ghost wanted us to, it seemed as if it must be all right. I reached into the desk and took out the book.

Setting it between us on the desk, I lifted the cover. I turned to see if the Woman in White was going to look over my shoulder or if she wanted us to make room between us, or what. It's very hard to know what you should do about manners when you're dealing with a ghost!

But before I could say anything, she faded out of sight.

"Well, I like that!" said Chris. "You'd think she—"

"Shhh!" I hissed. "She might still be here."

Chris looked around nervously. "I guess we'd better look this thing over and get out of here," she said.

I nodded my head and opened the book.

It was like taking a cushion off the couch and finding half a dozen pieces for the jigsaw puzzle you're working on. It didn't answer all our questions, but it sure gave us a lot more to work with.

"Well, you were right about one thing," said Chris when we had finished going through the book. "I thought it was going to be a scrapbook full of stuff about Pop. But it looks like it might be more about the theater itself."

I knew why that was bothering her. She was secretly convinced Pop was the one causing all the trouble. If the scrapbook had been all about him, it would have meant the ghost wanted us to know he was somehow connected to the mystery. But if it was just about the theater, then maybe there was something else in it the ghost wanted us to see. I had no idea which it was.

I turned back to the most important section, the pages filled with clippings about the tragedy that had taken place fifty years ago.

Because I had read the play so many times, it was interesting to read the newspaper accounts of what had *actually* happened on that terrible night—and in the days that followed, which the play didn't cover.

One of the articles had a picture of Lily in costume for the show. I think seeing it was one of the spookiest things that happened to me during this whole experience. I mean there was this woman looking out at me from the page of a fifty-year-old newspaper—the same woman I had seen just minutes before when she had led me to this room. She was even wearing the same dress!

But it was the pictures of the men that really bothered me. Both of them looked familiar for some reason. Several articles talked about how the men had been friends until they both fell in love with Lily.

"Did they get the wrong man?" Chris asked. "Maybe that's why the ghost is still here—she's waiting for justice to be done. She can't rest in peace until the man who killed her is hunted down."

"That was fifty years ago!" I said. "They could both be dead by now."

"Sure, but they could be alive, too. If they were twenty-five when it happened, they'd be seventy-five now. Lots of people make it that long. My grandfather's seventy-five, and he still runs his own business."

I looked at the pictures in the scrapbook—two handsome men and one beautiful woman. I wondered what had really happened between them.

"Yikes!" said Chris, glancing up at the clock over Pop's desk. "Look how late it is! We'd better get upstairs. They're probably wondering what happened to us."

"Or Pop might be on his way down here again," I said nervously. "You're right. Let's get going."

I put the scrapbook back in the desk, and we headed for the stairs.

We didn't get very far. We were a few steps into the storage room when we heard footsteps coming down the stairs toward us.

"It's Pop!" hissed Chris. "Go the other way! He'll kill us if he finds us down here."

I didn't have to be told twice. We turned and bolted in the opposite direction, past Pop's office and into the maze of tunnels that ran beneath the theater.

I wasn't sure if Chris meant Pop would really yell at us if he caught us down there—or if she really thought he'd kill us to keep us from telling what we had seen.

At the moment it didn't make that much difference. I just wanted to get away from him. I followed Chris into a dark corridor and bumped into her when she stopped short in front of me. "We should be safe now," she whispered.

I held my breath and listened, just in case. The footsteps were still coming! "Let's get out of here!" I hissed urgently.

Chris took my hand and began inching her way forward. I kept my other hand against the wall, so I could feel my way along. Chris was doing the same thing. Suddenly I heard her gasp.

A second later I, too, felt what had startled her. We had come to a slab of smooth metal that jutted out about six inches from the right-hand wall. As I ran my fingers over it, I felt crossbars and the heads of bolts. It was a large door.

About the time I figured out what it was, Chris pulled me through the opening.

"We should be safe in here," she whispered in my ear.

I didn't even answer. We huddled together, straining our ears to catch the sound of approaching footsteps.

For a moment there was nothing to be heard. But just as I was beginning to relax, I heard them again. They were still coming in our direction. I tightened my grip on Chris's arm, but didn't make a sound. It seemed entirely possible my life might depend on it.

"Oh, no!" hissed Chris. "He's got a flashlight!"

It was true. I could see the beam of light as it swept down the hallway in an arc, passing for a moment into our little room.

Trying desperately not to make a sound, we slid back against the wall as the footsteps drew nearer.

I wanted to scream and get it over with. I still don't know how I managed to keep quiet.

The footsteps stopped beside the doorway. I was shaking all over, waiting for the person to step through.

What happened next was even worse. No one stepped into the room. Instead the door slowly rolled shut. By the light of the flashlight, I could see that it was a huge slab, suspended by rollers from a bar above the doorway—like a sliding closet door, except about a hundred times as heavy.

I didn't know what to do. If I yelled to stop the door from closing, it might cost us our lives. If I kept my mouth shut, we would be sealed in, possibly for days. Possibly longer than we could last without food or water.

The choice was taken out of my hands. In less time than it takes to tell about it, the door slid into place with a thud. The footsteps went back down the hallway.

Chris and I were alone in the dark.

CHAPTER FIFTEEN

The Trap

We stood there for a few minutes, not moving, barely even breathing. I didn't know if it was because we were afraid Pop—or whoever it was out there—would come back, or because we were just so stunned at what had happened.

"Well," said Chris finally, "I guess we'd better see what we can do about getting out of here."

That sounded like a good idea to me, and I said so. However, it was one of those things that was easier said than done. We made three tries to open the door. As you might have suspected, it wouldn't budge.

"I was afraid of that," panted Chris, leaning against the door and gasping after our last effort.

I didn't even answer her. I was too tired, and too scared.

"Well, let's look the rest of this place over," she said.

I pointed out that it wasn't going to do much good to look anything over when it was totally dark. Chris responded that being picky wasn't going to get us anywhere. Actually, that was the *meaning* of what she said. Her actual words would probably burn this page.

We were both a little on edge. We apologized to each other and decided to stick together as we made our way around the room looking for another way out. The reason for staying together was simple. We had no idea how big the room was, or if there might be other rooms opening off it. I had a terrible vision of our getting separated and bouncing from wall to wall as we tried to find each other again.

As it turned out, the room wasn't all that big. In fact, it was small, which wouldn't have been so bad—if it hadn't been getting smaller!

I was the first one to notice it because I was standing, while Chris was slumped against the wall. I don't know what made me look up—a slight whirring sound, maybe. It didn't do me any good, of course. I couldn't see a thing. Acting on instinct, I reached up—and felt the ceiling coming down to meet me!

Well, enough is enough. I broke down and screamed. I mean, can you imagine it? I couldn't figure out what was going on. It was one thing to be trapped in that room. But we were in a theater, for heaven's sake, not in some old castle with secret rooms and traps for the enemies of the king.

Chris jumped up and clamped a hand over my mouth. "What do you think you're doing?" she hissed in my ear.

"Mmphepphmm," I said, which was the best I could manage with her hand over my mouth.

I was trying to figure out how to explain what was happening when the ceiling ran into us.

Chris screamed and dove to the floor, taking me with her. We rolled off to the side.

I started to laugh when I realized it wasn't the ceiling at all. It was a small wooden platform, part of a crude elevator of some sort.

How did I know, when it was pitch black?

Simple. It wasn't pitch black anymore. The Woman in White was standing on the platform. She had an aura of light around her. It wasn't bright; it was just a soft, gentle glow that let me make out what was happening.

The platform came to rest on the floor beside us. The ghost stepped off. She smiled at us, and I smiled back.

She made a gesture, indicating she wanted us to step onto the platform. We did.

She stood next to us, but not on the platform, and pointed to a switch. It had three positions: Up, Off, and Down. Right then it was pointing at Down.

Chris looked at me and raised an eyebrow. I shrugged. She reached out and flipped the switch to Up.

We took off as if we were on a rocket and hurtled toward the top of the shaft. When we looked up we both began to scream. We were approaching the ceiling of the shaft so fast that it didn't seem possible we could stop in time.

We didn't. But we didn't get squashed, either.

The shaft led to a trap door in the stage. An automatic device popped the trap, and we went shooting up through it like bread from a toaster, right into the middle of the rehearsal.

If I hadn't been so scared, it would have been one of the funniest moments of my life. As it was, it was still pretty funny. Melissa happened to be standing right in front of the spot where we came flying up through the floor. She let out a scream, jumped backward, landed in the middle of a group of singers, and sent them all tumbling to the floor.

It took about five minutes for the confusion to settle down and the yelling and screaming to begin. Edgar was as mad as anyone I'd ever seen. I think it was partly because he wasn't even sure what he wanted to be mad about. He was furious because we had disrupted rehearsal. But he was just as mad, he said, because we could have been killed, we could have hurt someone else, we had violated his trust, we were abusing equipment, and we were behaving like little savages. He kept jumping from point to point and getting madder as he did.

Things weren't improved any by the fact that Melissa was carrying on as though the little bruise she had on her elbow were a broken bone.

What finally saved us from all this was more trouble. I spotted Gwendolyn Meyer charging down the aisle. She had a large paper bag in her hand, and two policemen trailing along behind her.

I tried to let Edgar know what was coming. But he thought I was being sassy, and just got that much madder. He was interrupted by a bellow from Gwendolyn that probably shook the chandeliers.

"Don't anybody move!" she yelled, storming up onto the stage. "One of you people is trying to sabotage this show, and no one is going home until we find out who it is."

The cop behind her looked as if he wanted to take charge of the situation but wasn't quite sure how to do it. The cast and crew began shouting angry questions.

Chris and I took that moment to slip out of Edgar's sight and into the group.

Using her bullhorn voice, Gwendolyn got everyone to sit down. Then she stood on the edge of the stage and turned over the bag she was holding. A soggy mass of blackened paper fell to the floor with a splat.

"That," she said dramatically, "is all that's left of the publicity material for this show. Original press releases. Photographs. Scripts for television and radio spots. It was in my office, and it was fine at seven o'clock tonight when I locked the door. Half an hour ago I went in and found it on fire in my wastebasket. Now I want to know what happened, and I want to know now."

She fixed us all with a stare. No one stood up and confessed, which was hardly a surprise under the circumstances. Gwendolyn continued to glare anyway.

One of the cops stepped up behind her. "What I want to know is, who was out of this room for more than ten minutes tonight," he said.

My stomach sank. I figured Chris and I would be the first ones accused. But as it worked out, our

absence was no problem. *Everyone* had been out of
the room at one point or another.

"Well, who else has a key to your office,
ma'am?" asked the other policeman.

Gwendolyn looked frustrated. "No one," she
said. "There are only two keys. One is on my key
ring, and the other is kept in my desk drawer. No
one else has one."

"I hate to ask this," said Paula softly, "but
doesn't Pop have a set of master keys for the whole
building?"

"Of course he does," said Gwendolyn. "But it
couldn't have been him. He left the building at five
o'clock to have dinner with a friend. I don't expect
him back until after midnight."

I looked at Chris. She looked back, and I
could see that she was asking herself the same
question I was. If Pop was out of the building, who
had closed that door on us while we were
downstairs?

Unaware of this new mystery, Gwendolyn and
the police continued questioning the cast. They
were also unaware of the murmur that was
starting to ripple through the group. "It's the
ghost," people were whispering. "The ghost doesn't
want us to do the show!"

Some people were saying it as a joke. But a lot
of them really meant it.

I couldn't really blame them. After everything that had gone on, to have that material destroyed was just too much. Of course, it might not have bothered people quite so much if we weren't all aware of how secure Gwendolyn's office was. But we all remembered the night Lydia's dress got torn up and what Edgar had said about the street crazies who could get into the theater at any time. The whole situation had prompted Gwendolyn to take extra precautions to keep her office safe.

So in a way, she had set people up to believe it was the ghost when this happened. I guessed we would be losing a lot more cast members before another twenty-four hours went by.

Ken Abbott accidentally summed up the way people felt when he said, a little too loudly, "Well, it looks like the Woman in White has struck again." He meant it as a joke, to break the tension. But from the murmur that swept through the rest of the cast, you could tell a lot of people were taking him seriously.

That was when Gwendolyn played her trump card. "Smarten up, people," she shouted. "The Woman in White has nothing to do with this."

"How do you know?" asked Marilyn.

"Somehow I just don't think ghosts use matches from local restaurants," snapped Gwendolyn, holding up a half-empty matchbook.

"Whoever started the fire in my office dropped this while they were there. And I'll eat my hat if it was a ghost."

I was close enough to Gwendolyn that by squinting I could make out the design on the matchbook. It was from the Brass Elephant, the little bar and restaurant two blocks down from the theater.

I'd made a lot of mistakes that night. But I made the biggest one right then. The funny thing is, I didn't even know it at the time.

What did I do?

I gasped. That was all. Just a tiny little gasp. What's even stranger is that I wasn't even gasping about the matches. I was gasping because it had suddenly hit me who was causing all the trouble. Unfortunately, the reason didn't make any difference. That gasp, coming when it did, convinced the saboteur that I had figured everything out.

Actually, that was only half true. I knew *who* it was. But I still didn't know why.

But the mistake had been made. How serious was it? Fatal, as things worked out.

CHAPTER SIXTEEN

Balcony Scene

At six-thirty the next evening I stood outside the theater waiting for Chris to show up. She thought I was crazy when I told her who was causing all the trouble. But after I had told her my reasons, she agreed I might be right.

I opened the fat envelope I was holding and looked inside to make sure the papers were all there. It wasn't necessary, really. Nothing could have happened to them since the last time I checked. But it made me feel better to look. If I was going to take them to Gwendolyn as proof, I didn't want to take any chances.

I walked to the edge of the curb and looked in both directions. No sign of Chris.

I crossed back to the theater and stood reading the posters for the fifth time.

What could be keeping her? I wondered. I really wanted her to be with me when I turned my envelope of stuff over to Gwendolyn and told her what I had figured out.

I went back to the curb. No sign of her.

I couldn't stand out there any longer. I had to get someplace where I could sit and think. I wanted to make sure I had all my facts straight before I talked to Gwendolyn.

Pushing open the door to the lobby, I stepped into the theater. It seemed deserted. I knew that wasn't the case. I knew there were people working backstage, and at least one person in the box office. Even so, it seemed a little strange not to see anyone.

I decided to go up into the balcony. It was a good place to sit and think. I climbed the stairs and crossed the mezzanine without seeing anyone. Seconds later I was climbing toward the balcony. I remembered the first time I had gone up there. So much had happened since then!

Still clutching my envelope, I moved to the front of the balcony and sat down. I looked down at

the stage, vaguely hoping I might spot the Woman
in White. But she didn't seem to be around that
evening.

Sighing, I pulled the papers out of the
envelope and started going over them again.

They sure made it clear why Andrew Heron
and Edward Parker had looked so familiar when I
saw their picture in that old newspaper in Pop's
office.

It was funny. Even though I had heard Paula
mention it once, I hadn't realized how strong the
ties between theater people were until I had called
the library to ask for Sam, the hunk at the
reference desk. Of course I gave him a powerful
motive to help me out when I asked, "How would
you like to catch the person who stole your
microfilms?" But I had the feeling he would have
been glad to do it anyway.

I spent the rest of the day sitting around,
waiting for his call. When it finally came at four
o'clock and he told me what he had found out, I let
out a shout that should have rattled the windows.
The last pieces had fallen into place. Finally,
everything made sense.

I called my dad, then took the next bus
downtown, where I hurried to the library to pick
up the copies Sam had made and go over the
important points with him. Then, as I had worked
out with my father the night before, I called

Gwendolyn to ask if I could see her for a few minutes before rehearsal started. She was pretty cranky about it. But I think she was so happy I wasn't calling to quit that she agreed without too much fuss.

I looked at my watch. Just a few more minutes.

Where could Chris be?

Suddenly I heard footsteps behind me.

"It's about time!" I said, turning in my seat.

But it wasn't Chris. It was Lydia.

"Hello, Nine," she said pleasantly. "What are you doing here?"

"Just waiting for rehearsal," I said. "I got here a few minutes early. I like to come up here when I have the time. It's a good place to think."

"I'm afraid you think too much," said Lydia softly.

Her voice was perfectly sweet. But I knew from the look in her eyes that I was in trouble.

"I was hoping that when I locked you and your nosy little friend in that room underneath the stage, the two of you would get the message that so much snooping around could be bad for your health. If you had, we might not be having this unpleasant little meeting right now."

Yep. There was no doubt about it. I was in *big* trouble!

"But then, maybe it was already too late," said Lydia, sliding into the seat next to me. "Tell me—what was it about that matchbook that tipped you off? Most of the cast hangs out at the Brass Elephant. I can't figure out why you connected it to me."

"I didn't," I said truthfully.

"Don't lie to me!" said Lydia, her eyes blazing. "I heard you gasp. I saw the look on your face."

"But that didn't have anything to do with the matchbook," I said. "I just happened to figure things out right then."

What a mouth! I might have gotten away with it if I had just stuck with my story that seeing the matchbook hadn't tipped me off to anything. Which was true, almost: the matchbook made me think of Lydia, because of seeing her and Alan at the Brass Elephant earlier that day. But it certainly wasn't what solved the mystery for me.

Of course, with what Lydia had already said by this point, keeping quiet probably wouldn't have made any difference. I knew, and she knew that I knew, and so on.

I was getting pretty nervous.

"Well, what was it?" she asked persistently. "How *did* you figure out it was me?"

"Gwendolyn's office," I said tersely.

"I don't understand."

"You tried to blame the ghost one time too many. Since I knew it wasn't the ghost causing the trouble, it had to be someone human. So I asked myself who could have gotten into Gwendolyn's office besides her or Pop. It seemed that it was impossible—until I remembered the night your dress got ripped up. Or should I say the night *you* tore up your dress, and blamed it on the ghost?"

"Say whatever you want," said Lydia. "Just get on with it."

"Well, I remembered that Gwendolyn had asked Ken Abbott to take you to her office so you could lie down. No matter what else I think of you, I have to admit you're a pretty good actress. You had to be, to pull off all that screaming hysteria and make it seem real. Anyway, you were in there alone for a long time—plenty of time to get a key out of Gwendolyn's desk drawer."

"Very clever," Lydia said. "But that's not evidence. Someone else might have been in there that you didn't know about."

"True," I said. "But it all just fell into place after that. I might not have figured it out if I hadn't seen the ghost myself—"

"You didn't!" said Lydia sharply.

"Oh, but I did. Several times. So I knew what she was like. That was why I couldn't buy your story about all the trouble she was causing. Then I realized that all we had to go on was your word. You were the one who was disrupting things, with your claims that the ghost was after you. Who had a better chance to rip up that dress than you yourself? Once I figured out the bit about the key, it all fell into place.

"Except I still couldn't figure out why—until I thought about your name. Suddenly the coincidence seemed too much. Andrew Heron was convicted of the murder of Lily Larkin. Lydia Crane is starring in a play about that murder. Crane and Heron, Heron and Crane. The names went round and round in my mind, until I remembered that heron and crane are two different names for the same bird. But then, I'm sure you already know that, don't you—Lydia *Heron*?"

Lydia stood up. I thought she was going to hit me. Instead she reached for the envelope.

"No!" I said, without thinking how dangerous it might be to try to stop her. "You can't have it."

"Oh, but I most certainly can," Lydia said. She grabbed me by the arms and pushed me against the edge of the balcony.

"Let go!" I screamed. "Let go of me!"

She continued pushing me sideways over the balcony. I struggled, but I was afraid that even if I managed to break free I would lose my balance and fall over.

"Let the child be!" said a gruff voice from behind Lydia.

It was Pop. Chris was standing next to him, out of breath and looking terrified.

"You stay out of this, old man!" screeched Lydia.

"I said let the child be!" roared Pop as he came charging down the aisle.

Lydia pushed me aside and turned to face him. "Get away from me," she screamed. "Get away from me, you murderer!"

Pop stopped in his tracks.

"It wasn't me, Lydia," he said. "It wasn't me, and you know it wasn't. Your father was the man who killed Lily Larkin. He killed her and left me here to wait for her."

"He didn't!" screamed Lydia. "He didn't! He didn't! You did it, and they blamed him! You ruined his life, and I'm not going to let this show stir all that up again."

And with that she threw herself at Pop, scratching and clawing and hitting as if she had gone out of her mind.

They fought for a moment at the edge of the balcony. Then Lydia took a wild swing at Pop, missed, and lost her balance. She fell against the railing. He reached out to help her, she grabbed his hand, and they went over the edge together.

CHAPTER SEVENTEEN

Curtain Call

With the mystery of who was trying to sabotage the show solved, *The Woman in White* went on to become a smashing success. We replaced Lydia with Marilyn. The cast pulled together to make up for the time we lost. And the publicity brought us a full house on opening night. "There's lots of bad news," said Gwendolyn smugly. "But very little bad publicity."

I guess she was right, because tickets started going like crazy as soon as the story hit the papers.

Opening night was incredible. I suppose it might have had something to do with what we had all been through together. Whatever the reason, the cast seemed to catch fire that night, and the show came to life in a way I had never thought possible. It was as though we were all actually *living* the story. I'll never forget standing in front of that audience at the end and feeling the love from all those hundreds of shouting, stamping, applauding people who were thanking us for making them laugh, for making them cry.

It was an incredible experience.

But one other experience in the old Grand Theater that summer burned even more deeply into my heart. It happened the night after Pop died trying to save my life.

I had sneaked into the balcony again, to be alone, to think about what had happened to him, and to me. I thought about all the years of sorrow and anger that had ended that night, years I had figured out through the research Sam the librarian did for me the day of that final disaster.

Sam explained his techniques to me later— how he used the names and information I had given him to comb through old newspapers and county records to put together the picture that finally made sense of it all.

It was Sam who gave me the big picture. But the details came from Lydia herself. She had survived the fall from the balcony, although not without several broken bones. When the police came to the hospital to question her about the accident, she broke down and confessed everything.

It was fairly simple, really. In 1935 Andrew Heron was convicted of the murder of Lily Larkin. Twenty-six years later, in 1961, he was released from prison on parole. A year later he married a younger woman whom he had convinced of his innocence. Together they had a baby: Lydia Heron.

Lydia and her father were similar in both temperament and appearance. Which was why Andrew looked so familiar to me when I saw his picture that time; he was like a male version of his daughter. Lydia had also inherited Andrew's talent, and he taught her everything he knew about theater and acting. But at the same time he was filling her with stories about the great injustice that he felt had been done to him. He gave her both his talent, and his enormous bitterness toward Edward Parker, the man who had won Lily Larkin's affections.

Mistakenly believing her father was innocent, it became Lydia's goal to clear his name. She wanted to eliminate anything that connected him to the crime—which was why she stole the microfilm from the library. Unfortunately for her, she didn't think of that until after the announcement had gone out that the Grand Theater was mounting a play based on the Lily Larkin story.

When Lydia heard about the play, she knew she had to stop it. With her theatrical training, it was easy enough to get a part, although she had been somewhat surprised when she landed the lead. Once she was in the play, her plan to force it to a halt by making it look like the ghost was disrupting things just seemed to come naturally, and she went at it from every angle she could think of. The day Chris and I spotted her going into the Brass Elephant with Alan, she had been trying to convince the poor guy that he should give up on his script because the Woman in White was so opposed to the show.

What Lydia hadn't counted on was that the Woman in White herself would take over.

And Pop? On the night Lily Larkin died in his arms, Edward Parker vowed to give up his acting career and stay at the Grand Theater until he and Lily were reunited. In time people forgot who he was, and why he was there, and just started calling him "Pop." Occasionally a famous performer who remembered Edward Parker from his acting days would come to town with a show and go down to Pop's little office to share a few beers and some memories. That was where all those autographed pictures had come from.

For fifty years Pop stayed at the Grand, waiting to be reunited with Lily. I thought about the night we had seen him sitting in the third row, crying. I wondered if it was because we could see the ghost and he couldn't.

Now, as I sat there staring at the stage, I heard a familiar strain of music—a waltz filled with sweetness and unbearable longing. It was the song the Woman in White always danced to: "The Heart That Stays True."

Looking down on the stage, I saw her for the last time. She was dancing in slow, sweeping circles, her empty arms held out before her. Again that feeling of sadness swept over me, and I could feel the tears start to run down my cheeks.

But a moment later everything changed. The music picked up speed, becoming livelier and sweeter.

And then a man stepped onto the stage, tall and handsome and filled with life, even though he was obviously a ghost, too.

It was a man I had seen before, in a picture in a newspaper fifty years old.

It was Pop—Edward Parker—the way he had looked on the day Lily died.

Crossing to the Woman in White, he took her in his arms, and they began to dance together. He whirled her around the floor, and her dress swept out behind her. The music began to swell, louder and faster and sweeter than ever. It seemed their feet were barely touching the floor.

I thought I was going to go out of my skin with the joy of it all.

And then, almost before it had begun, it was over. Still whirling around and around the stage, they began to fade slowly from my sight. A moment later they were gone. Only one note of music was left, a sweet pure note that hung in the air after they had vanished.

And then it, too, was gone, and there was nothing but an empty stage.

I sat there with tears streaming down my face, happier than I had ever thought possible.

ABOUT THE AUTHOR

BRUCE COVILLE has written over a dozen books for young readers, including *Sarah's Unicorn, The Monster's Ring, Eyes of the Tarot,* and *Waiting Spirits*. He has also written three musical plays for young audiences. His love of theater is part of what prompted him to write *The Ghost in the Third Row.*

Mr. Coville lives in Syracuse, New York, and has two children. Before becoming a full-time writer, he worked as a magazine editor, a teacher, a toymaker and a gravedigger.

WELCOME TO GALAXY HIGH* . . .

A school asteroid far out, way out and spaced out in time . . .

—Where the class president is a six-armed Venutian!
—The class gossip has five mouths that never take a break!
—The girls' gym teacher is a whiz at track—she's half horse!
—The local pizza parlor is as close as the nearest satellite!
—The school sport is like hockey—but the puck is alive!

And that's just the beginning! Join Doyle and Aimee, the new kids from Earth, as they encounter a zany collection of cosmic coeds from all over the universe!

Coming September 1987!

*Based on the television series "GALAXY HIGH SCHOOL," a production of TMS Entertainment, Inc.

FROM THE SPOOKY, EERIE PEN OF JOHN BELLAIRS . . .

☐ **THE CURSE OF THE**   **15540/$2.95**
BLUE FIGURINE

Johnny Dixon knows a lot about ancient Egypt and curses and evil spirits—but when he finds the blue figurine, he actually "sees" a frightening, super-natural world. Even his friend Professor Childermass can't help him!

☐ **THE MUMMY, THE WILL**   **15498/$2.75**
AND THE CRYPT

For months Johnny has been working on a riddle that would lead to a $10,000 reward. Feeling certain that the money is hidden somewhere in the house of a dead man, Johnny goes into his house where a bolt of lightning reveals to him that the house is not quite deserted . . .

☐ **THE SPELL OF THE**   **15357/$2.50**
SORCERER'S SKULL

Johnny Dixon is back, but this time he's not teamed up with Dr. Childermass. That's because his friend, the Professor, has disappeared!

Buy them at your local bookstore or use this handy coupon for ordering:

Bantam Books, Inc., Dept. SK3, 414 East Golf Road, Des Plaines, Ill. 60016

Please send me the books I have checked above. I am enclosing $_____ (please add $1.50 to cover postage and handling. Send check or money order—no cash or C.O.D.s please).

Mr/Ms _____

Address _____

City _____ State/Zip _____

SK3—7/87

Please allow four to six weeks for delivery. This offer expires 1/88.
Price and availability subject to change without notice.

☐ THE SARA SUMMER   15481/$2.50
by Mary Downing Hahn
Twelve-year-old Emily Sherwood has grown like a beanstalk and all the kids are calling her "Giraffe." What's worse, her best friend has deserted her. Things seem pretty bad until Sara, a tall, tough, wacky and wise New Yorker teaches Emily a thing or two about life.

☐ YOU'RE GOING OUT THERE A   15272/$2.25
KID, BUT YOU'RE COMING BACK A STAR
by Linda Hirsch
Margaret Dapple is ten years old and tired of waiting around to grow up, tired of waiting for everyone—especially her parents and big sister Barbara—to recognize that she is not a baby anymore. So Margaret decides to show them all—she's going to improve her image.

☐ NOW IS NOT TOO LATE   15548/$2.75
by Isabelle Holland
When Cathy arrives on the island to spend the summer with her grandmother, her summer friends warn her to stay away from the Wicked Witch, who turns out to be hauntingly familiar and not a witch at all.

☐ THE SISTERS IMPOSSIBLE   26013/$2.50
by J. D. Landis
As sisters go, Saundra and Lily have never been the best of friends. But the real trouble starts when their father buys younger sister Lily a pair of dancing shoes so she can go to ballet school with the beautiful and accomplished Saundra.

☐ ANASTASIA KRUPNIK   15534/$2.75
by Lois Lowry
To Anastasia Krupnik, being ten is very confusing. On top of everything her parents are going to have a baby—at their age! It's enough to make a kid want to do something terrible . . .